Erotica 1:
Bettina's Tales

D1639287

Erotica 1:
Bettina's Tales

collected by
Bettina Varese

**THE
COLLECTIVE**

Copyright © THE COLLECTIVE PUBLISHING COMPANY

First published in 1999 by
THE COLLECTIVE PUBLISHING COMPANY

ISBN 0 9535290 0 2

All rights reserved. No part of this publication may be reproduced,
stored in a retrieval system, or transmitted, in any form or by any means
without the prior written permission of the publisher, nor be otherwise
circulated in any form of binding or cover other than that in which
it is published, and without a similar condition being
imposed on the subsequent purchaser.

All characters and all events are purely fictitious,
and any resemblance real or fancied to actual
persons or events is entirely coincidental.

Stories by Bettina Varese
Edited by Eliza Croft, Judy Keaton & Simon Starkwell
Designed and Typeset by The Collective

Printed and bound in Great Britain
by Cox and Wyman Ltd
Reading, Berkshire

THE COLLECTIVE
P.O. Box 10, Sunbury on Thames, TW16 7YG
United Kingdom

THE
COLLECTIVE

ENGLAND

Bettina writes,

I always carry a condom wherever I go.
Make sure you also practise safe sex.

Contents

Contents

Contents

Dear Reader,

First of all may I welcome you to my collection of stories. I hope that you find them as hot and sexy as I do. When I read them, my pussy always gets really wet, and I end up having to change my panties, but not before I've fingered myself to a delicious orgasm. On one occasion I got through several pairs, and I had to go out without any on. But that's another story!

Hope you enjoy them,

Much love,

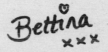

Bettina writes,

A few years ago, while I was at Drama School, I met a girl called Natalie. We became good friends, and shared a flat in St. John's Wood. We lost touch for a year or so, and then recently I bumped in to her in Knightsbridge. We had a lot to catch up on and spent a weekend together. We reminisced about old times, and I asked her if I could put some of her experiences in my books. The story coming up is one of them.

The Dinner Party

THE DINNER PARTY

Before I tell you my story, I'd better introduce myself. My name is Natalie and I'm a drama student. I love to meet interesting people as I am also a student of life. I observe and absorb everything, and this helps me to develop my characters when I'm acting.

Recently I met Pierre. He is beautiful, and articulate, and knows so many things. Whenever we spend time together I know I am going to have a good time. When I am with him, I realise there is so much in life I know nothing about. But Pierre loves to teach me. He says I'm a great pupil.

Take last weekend for instance. Pierre took me to a party to meet some of his friends. When we first arrived, I was surprised at the affection they showered on us, welcoming us with hugs and kisses. They seemed very warm and friendly, and I was flattered by the interest they showed in me. There were no painful silences, and they appeared genuinely happy to meet someone new. I was given a large glass of cool, white wine, and shown to a chair, which I sank into next to a very glamourous woman. She smiled, and began to ask me questions about my acting. All the time she was talking to me, I found myself drawn to her large blue eyes, which looked into mine attentively. She sat in a seductive pose with one leg tucked neatly behind the other. I felt myself blush as my eyes wandered slowly up and down her lithe and sensuous form. When at last the spell broke, I looked around at the other guests. They too were very beautiful people, who sat in elegance around a low coffee table in the centre of the room. The low hum of their chatter seemed to hypnotise me, and I glanced from face to face, and then from top to toe, of everyone present.

One woman stood up and introduced Pierre and myself to the five others. I guessed that she had to be our host, Sara. She was stunning, with long auburn hair, a wonderful figure, and Betty Grable legs. I could see by Pierre's body language that he was obviously attracted to her. I continued to look around at the other guests. Next to Sara, were a handsome couple who sat close to each other, with their bodies touching. He was rugged, with piercing blue-violet eyes and short cropped hair. She was darker, but also had short hair that gave her an elfin appearance, and her figure was delicate and boyish. They were introduced as Della and Mark. The next couple were Suzanne and Michael. It was Suzanne's birthday and the party was being thrown for her. She was the hypnotizing woman who had spoken to me when I first arrived. Her husband, Michael, was tall, and had as much, if not more, style than Suzanne. He was blonde, tanned, and gorgeous, and I could hardly bare to look away from him. His strong muscled legs stretched out in front of him, and his eyes twinkled as he caught my gaze. They were the most dazzling eyes I think I've ever seen, and his golden yellow hair just shone like an angel's. I was totally mesmerised. When I looked to my left, there was a good-looking man who was introduced as Ralph, Sara's husband. He took my hand to his lips and kissed it gently. It felt very sensual and I didn't want to pull my hand away.

As the evening progressed, we ate, and talked, and drank, as if we had all been friends forever. As we drank more and more, I realised that I was becoming very aroused. This was one of the strangest situations I had ever found myself in. Everybody in the room seemed sensual, in a way that I had not been aware of before. I couldn't wait to be alone with Pierre, and I knew that sex would be on the agenda. I also knew that I desired Ralph, and that I would fantasize about his dark looks as Pierre took me in his arms.

At some point in the proceedings, Sara appeared with ready rolled joints, which we all took gladly. Then the combination of the sickly sweet smoke, the weed itself, and the alcohol, began to take effect. Everybody seemed to become less inhibited, and the conversation turned to sexual matters.

Suzanne removed all the glasses and ash trays from the coffee table. Then, as if it were a perfectly normal thing to do, she lay across it letting her arms and legs fall gently at each corner. Judging from the reactions of the others, this was not unusual. Ralph reached behind his chair and brought out some rope, which he shared out. Then, with help from the others, he carefully tied Suzanne to each leg of the table. I was transfixed. My eyes seemed glued to the sight before me. Suzanne was wearing nothing more than stockings under her short skirt. I could see a small triangle of beautiful pubic hair. Immediately I felt aroused, and I looked towards Pierre who was smiling at me.

He knew all along. He knew that this was no ordinary dinner party. I was shocked, but at the same time, I could feel that hot, slippery feeling between my legs that gave away my delight at this situation. I suddenly realised that I was immensely turned on by the sight of this erotic woman laid out before me.

Sara blindfolded Suzanne, and then kissed her on the lips as you would a lover. Della and Mark were either side of Suzanne. They began to unbutton her blouse, and unclip her bra which was fastened at the front. The blouse and the bra fell open, revealing her firm, pert breasts. Della and Mark gently licked her nipples. Sarah beckoned to me to join in. I hesitated because of embarrassment. I didn't want to do anything, as I wasn't quite sure what was expected. But, deep down inside I knew that there weren't any barriers, barring those I made for myself. I wanted to touch those warm thighs that lay in front of me. I wanted to see what a woman's pussy tasted like, but I was restrained by guilt. I had never been aroused by a woman before, apart from erotic pictures which Pierre often showed me.

I was trying to debate all the issues, when Pierre said, "Don't you want to touch?"

Hesitantly I approached the coffee table, and I knelt in front of Suzanne. Then, I felt my inhibitions begin to drift away. Softly, I ran my fingers up her thighs towards that heavenly place between her legs, and I felt her muscles tighten expectantly. I let my hand linger over her pussy. I glanced up to where Pierre sat, and he was looking at me approvingly. So, I leaned forward and licked her with my tongue, teasing her clitoris. She let out a little cry of delight. My tongue gently explored her pussy as I tasted a woman for the first time. While I continued to suck and tease Suzanne, I saw Della remove her panties and throw them to Pierre, who tucked them in his pocket. He watched as she climbed on to the table and lowered her pussy down on to Suzanne's face. Della moaned with pleasure as she gently moved backwards and forwards over Suzanne's open mouth. I suddenly felt a strong, warm hand slip between my breasts, and I didn't fight it as I turned to find Ralph behind me. Deftly with his other hand he removed my blouse, and undid my bra which slipped to the floor, leaving my breasts cold and exposed but without shame. I glanced across to Pierre, and he was watching me intently. I pulled Ralph's head towards my erect nipples, and offered one up to his receptive mouth. I was overcome with a desire that I hoped Pierre couldn't see. Ralph sucked my nipple, and played with it until it hurt. Then, lifting my skirt and pulling off my panties, he pushed me back into a chair. My view of Pierre was obscured by Ralph's large cock as he thrust it into my face. I cupped his balls in my hand and began teasing him with my tongue, running it up and down his shaft, as his erect penis tried desperately to get between my lips. My tongue darted on and off it several times, teasing him. I could feel him getting more and more excited, wanting to be inside my mouth. Then, I quickly took it into my mouth right up to it's hilt, and tasted it. I felt him shudder with delight, as I bit gently into his rock hard penis. As I let it move in and out of my mouth, I felt warm hands sliding up my thighs towards my hot pussy, and I arched my back away from the chair to give them more access. Then I realised someone was pushing between my legs to reach their tongue into my hole, which ached with desire. The long tongue slipped into my glistening pussy and sucked gently. I felt them expertly find my clitoris. My whole body was tingling with pleasure as never before. Ralph started to groan, and as his cock began to spasm in my mouth, cum spurted into my throat. I swallowed as much as I could, but some dripped out of my mouth and ran down my chin on to my breasts. As he pulled away from me, I looked down to see Sara's auburn hair, and I became aware that for the first time I was being eaten by a woman. A woman who knew exactly what to do to me, as only a woman could. It was such a turn on to see Sara's head between my legs. She gazed up at me, her eyes alight with sensuous delight. I sighed, and caressed her hair, as she plunged her tongue again into my pussy. Mark, who had been sitting next to Pierre watching for a while, came over and knelt down behind Sara. He unzipped his fly and took out his erect penis. He parted her legs, and pushed his cock inside her cunt. He watched it as it went in and out of her, and she moaned with delight still licking my pussy out. As I watched him fuck her, as she was eating me, I was ready to come. The room began to spin, and I put my fingers in my mouth to stifle my screams as my climax ripped through me. I pushed Sara's head away, and her hands pressed down on the floor, while Mark still pounded her from behind. I lowered myself to kiss her, and her orgasm began. Her mouth stayed open as she came. I squeezed her nipples between my fingers as her ecstasy reached it's peak. Mark withdrew from her and his cum shot across her arse and back.

We looked over to the coffee table where Della was finger fucking Suzanne. As she worked on her pussy, Michael positioned himself over Suzanne's face, and filled her mouth with his enormous erection, stopping her ecstatic moans from escaping, and his body writhed as his cock strained to fill her entire mouth gagging her cries. Sara and I sat back and watched them.

Della moved across to where Pierre was sitting. She began to rub his cock through his trousers. Pierre unzipped his fly, and Della reached in, to pull his erect penis towards her mouth. She ran her tongue up and down it's shaft, holding it's base in her hand. It disappeared into her mouth. I expected to feel jealous of my man being touched by another woman, but it only sent more waves of lust through my body. Della lifted herself up, and sat astride his lap with his penis still gripped in her hand. She guided it into her waiting pussy, and pushed herself down on to it. She arched her body, and threw her head back as she rode up and down on him. Both her hands rubbed her clit, and I thought she was going to come, but instead she got off, and again took his cock in her mouth. As she sucked harder and harder he began to come in her mouth. She withdrew her mouth from his cock, and it spurted cum all over her tits. She got up and stood with her legs apart, leaning back against the wall. She began to slowly massage the cum over her tits with one hand, while she rubbed her clitoris with the other. She was really getting off on the fact that we were all watching her. Her tits were covered with creamy white spunk, and her dress was up around her waist. I was getting really turned on, and so was Sara who began to touch herself as she sat beside me. Della turned around, leaned her arms against the wall, and stuck out her arse expectantly. Mark automatically came to her, and pushed his prick into her from behind. She immediately began to come. He ran his hands up and down her body as he pushed her against the wall. She screamed out. He felt her sticky, cum-drenched breasts with his large strong hands, and fingered her clit as she came powerfully in his arms.

The clock chimed midnight. Sara got up and told everyone it was time for Suzanne to get her birthday wish. Suzanne was untied and her blindfold removed. Smoothing out her skirt, she sat on the edge of the coffee table. She looked around the room at each of us in turn, and when her blue eyes fell on me, she walked over and took my hand.

She led me to the large Edwardian day bed in front of the bay window. She lay down on it and opened her legs. The day bed was low enough for her to be able to put her feet on the floor at either side. She pulled her skirt up, and said to me, "Natalie, please will you kiss my pussy?"

I knelt on the floor, and parted her lips with my fingertips. I lightly kissed the rose red flesh. Slowly, I licked round and round the tight opening, and her breathing became heavy and fast. At that moment I would have done anything she asked. She was so beautiful, and I was the one who was giving her pleasure. I had my hands on her inner thighs, caressing them gently, just above the stocking tops. As my tongue slipped in and out, and up and down, her bottom lifted to push her pussy further into my mouth.

Suzanne said, "Michael, come over here. I want to see you fucking Natalie, while I can see her beautiful face licking my pussy."

I felt Michael's hands on my bottom and he eased my legs apart. Then, I felt his strong hand between my legs, and a finger slid into my cunt. I was already soaking wet, so it was easy for him to push his stiff penis in as far as it would go. He began slowly to fuck me, and I looked up at Suzanne. She was looking straight at me. Our eyes were transfixed, and I sucked harder on her clit. Then I began to mimic the rhythm of Michael's cock pushing into me. I could see Suzanne getting more and more excited. She was opening her legs as far as she could, so I could go even deeper into her pussy with my tongue. Suzanne began to orgasm, wriggling and gripping my head between her thighs. Michael, seeing his wife in ecstasy, began to thrust harder and faster into me, his hands pulling my hips towards him. My body shuddered as I reached my climax. I felt Michael's hot cum shoot into me. All three of us came almost simultaneously through the sheer eroticism of the moment.

The guests began to tidy themselves up, and became respectable once more. They talked about when they might all get together again. Pierre and I gathered our coats from Sara's bedroom. Suzanne was in there, putting on some more lipstick. She enquired as to the date of my birthday. I told her it was next month. As we said our goodbyes, everyone kissed and embraced us, saying how much fun it had been.

Bettina writes,

My girlfriend Katie has a flat in London. She runs a phone sex service. She makes quite a lot of money out of it and has regular clients who ring her once a week, some once a day! Last time I visited her she was taking calls, and the next story is one of them.

I taped it on the extension line in her bedroom. I love to hear people talking dirty to each other, it really turns me on, and Katie is so good at it. She really knows which buttons to press and her voice is really sexy. When she had finished the calls I was feeling hot and frustrated. I made sure Katie turned her attention to me.

The Phone Call

THE PHONE CALL

"Hello, who is calling?"

"Hi, I'm Tony!"

"Hi Tony, this is Katie. Are you a first time caller?"

"Yes."

"And you are over eighteen aren't you?"

"Yeah, I'm twenty-one."

"Ooh twenty-one. I bet you're always ready for sex, aren't you Tony?"

"Yes."

"Would you like to know what I'm doing?"

"Yes please."

"Well Tony, I am sitting here in my stockings, suspenders and black lace panties. On my beautifully firm, rounded breasts, I'm wearing a sheer black bra. I'm thinking about sex. What are you doing Tony?"

"Um, I'm looking at your picture in a magazine and you are really turning me on."

"Tony, would you like me to tell you what I'm doing now?"

"Yeah, sure would."

"I'm stroking my nipples through my bra, and they are getting really hard. "

"Have you got big breasts?"

"Yes, big and firm Tony, they're 38D."

"So I could rub myself off between them and come all over your tits."

"Yeah I'd love that Tony."

"What are you doing now?"

"I'm running my hand up my thigh, and I'm slipping my fingers inside my panties. I'm fingering myself Tony. I'm imagining you fingering me Tony. Would you like to finger me Tony? Would you like to push your fingers deep into my cunt?"

"Yes please. Pull your panties down Katie."

"I'm pulling them down. The crotch is soaking wet. I'm taking off my panties now. Would you like to smell them Tony?"

"Yeah I would."

"Mmm, they smell of sex Tony. I could post them to you so that you could play with them when you look at my photo."

"Cool, would you do that? Can you rub your pussy for me and tell me how you turn yourself on."

"Tony, I'm rubbing my pussy and sliding my fingers in and out. Ummm. That feels really good. It's making me really wet. What do you look like, are you sexy Tony?"

"I think so. I'm tall and dark and I have big strong muscles. Does that sound good?"

"Good for me Tony. I could rub your strong chest, and I'd press my breasts into your back. I'll tell you how I get aroused. I like to touch myself. I'm doing it now Tony. My fingers are playing with my pussy. It's very warm and wet. I'd love you to get your tongue down there. Do you like pussy Tony?"

"Oh wow, I'd like to eat you and lick out those juices Katie. You are making my cock so hard. I'm holding it now. I wish I could push it into your wet cunt."

"Well Tony, I'm thinking about you doing just that, and my fingers are right inside me. Oh I'm so wet . . . . ooh . . ooh! I'm licking my juices and I'm playing with my clit. I'm rubbing it really hard. Would you like to play with my clit Tony?"

"Oh, yes, please. My dick is throbbing to come inside you, I want to fuck you so hard Katie!"

"Listen Tony, I'm coming hard, so hard and I can feel your huge prick inside me. Oh yes, push it in further, and harder. Oh Tony are you coming too? Let it happen Tony, oh yes . . oh . . oh . . it's now Tony. Can you feel my hot pussy holding on tight to your cock?"

"Oh yes Katie. I want to suck your tits. I want to play with your pussy and eat it up."

"Tony, rub yourself harder now. Are you coming?"

"Yeah, now, now . . ."

"Let it happen, just let that cum spurt on to my photo. All over me, on my face, in my mouth so I can taste it. Ummmm. Yeah it tastes lovely. That's it, keep going. Let it gush out . . ."

"My spunk is all over your face."

"Yeah, you really taste good . . . did you enjoy that Tony?"

"God Katie it was brilliant. Thanks babe. Can I ring you again soon?"

"Anytime Tony, anytime. I'll be here waiting for you with a wet pussy."

"Great, bye Katie."

"Bye Tony."

"Hello, who is calling?"

"Hi, I'm Simon!"

"Hi Simon, this is Katie. Would you like to know what I'm doing?"

"Yes please."

Bettina writes,

I get lots of letters and stories sent to me from bored housewives, who fantasize about having a bit of excitement in their lives. I have chosen this story, 'Reflections', because it's one of my favourites. As you may know, I love to hear and read about two-girl sex. I keep coming back to this story to read it again, so that I can imagine myself and a beautiful girl doing what these two get up to. It really turns me on when a woman takes the initiative and instigates sex.

Reflections

REFLECTIONS

Rachel was feeling relieved. The summer holidays were over and her children had returned to school just that morning. She had got the children up, made sure they had washed, had breakfast and got to the school bus on time. Now she was sitting alone in the kitchen, with her hands wrapped around a warm mug filled with strong coffee. It was just what she needed to give her a push to begin the rest of her day. Her husband had left early to attend a conference up in Nottingham. He was a paper-clip executive. She longed to be as important to him as his paper-pushing job, but he seemed to treat her like a house-keeper instead of a lover. She glanced through the door into the utility room, and sighed as she saw the mountainous pile of laundry she had collected from her children's bedrooms that morning. She also had a mound of ironing to do, as well as her weekly fight round the isles of the local supermarket. None of these activities seemed particularly enthralling, she thought, as she sipped the last of her coffee, and placed the empty mug into the sink alongside sticky cutlery, plates, and two cereal bowls half-filled with chocolate-coloured milk and soggy rice-pops.

She climbed the stairs lethargically, and gently side-stepped the damp towel which lay on the landing. Once in her bedroom she began to make the bed. But she had no enthusiasm for housework today, or any day. It bored her rigid to keep the house presentable, and she longed to do something more adventurous. As she straightened the sheets, her eye was drawn to her image in the full length mirror on the wardrobe. She didn't look bad for her age, she thought. Her shoulder-length, honey-blonde hair was soft and flattering, and she had a golden tan left over from a summer holiday in Greece. As she looked herself up and down, patting her flat tummy, she certainly didn't feel like a wife and mother. She still had an hourglass figure. Her breasts were still full and round, and she had nipples that usually stood out, which in some situations she found rather embarrassing. As she undid her dressing gown, letting it slip to the floor, she stroked her smooth skin. This made her feel warm and desirable. As she looked into the mirror, she flicked her hair back, pouting in what she hoped was a sexy manner. What a waste, when her husband couldn't even care less. She could count on one hand the number of times he had made love to her in the last month.

Just then, she heard a noise, and her trance was broken as a voice called out "Rachel, are you upstairs?"

"Yes" she cried as she hurriedly picked up her dressing gown, and she was just doing up the last button when her friend Chloe walked into the room.

"Aren't you dressed yet?" she said, "I thought, as it was our first day without the kids, we could do something exciting."

Rachel blushed like a shy schoolgirl caught doing something she shouldn't. She knew her face was flushed and this made her giggle.

"What were you up to?" asked Chloe smiling.

Rachel felt herself blush some more. "I was looking at myself naked in the mirror, to see whether I needed to take up your offer of a session down the gym."

"Did you like what you saw?" said Chloe, coming closer and gently touching Rachel's shoulders. "Let me see too," she said, playfully removing the dressing gown, which fell into a heap round Rachel's feet.

Both women looked in the mirror. Rachel noticed how Chloe's tight blouse accentuated the shape of her bosom. The blouse tucked into a short, blue skirt, and as it was a warm day her legs were bare. On her feet were high black peep toe sandals. Rachel had always envied Chloe's overt sexuality, which attracted men like moths to a flame. Rachel looked away. She had never thought of her friend in a sexual way before, but as their eyes had met, it was obvious what was on both their minds.

Chloe was the one to chance rejection. She kissed Rachel's now red lips. A shiver ran through Rachel's body, but to her surprise, it was not one of disgust, more of anticipation. They kissed passionately, and Chloe began to touch.

"I've never been with a woman, I don't know . . ." Rachel stammered.

"Sssh," whispered Chloe, as her hand began to probe it's way in between Rachel's legs, gently brushing against

25

her clitoris. "Don't say anything, just relax and let it happen."

She gently pushed Rachel's willing body on to the bed. Parting her friend's legs she began to run her hands up the soft golden thighs. Chloe's fingers reached Rachel's pussy again. Teasingly, her finger circled Rachel's clitoris, not touching it's tip. Rachel began to writhe with delight. Chloe licked Rachel's already erect nipples, then kissed her mouth, returning to the nipples and sucking again.

Chloe pulled up her skirt so as to straddle Rachel. With her hand behind her, she could continue to tease Rachel's clitoris, tantalizing her with light touches, whilst pushing her thumb into her own cunt through her panties. Rachel moaned with pleasure at Chloe's touch and begged, "Rub my clit Chloe, now.. " But, Chloe made her wait. She took her hand away and pushed two wet fingers into Rachel's mouth. Rachel sucked them, pretending they were an erect penis. Chloe moved down Rachel's body sliding her hands underneath the plump tanned buttocks. Rachel instinctively opened her legs, lifting them over to rest outside of Chloe's arms. Chloe pulled Rachel's open sex towards her mouth, and began to suck her clitoris. With her head moving up and down between the bronzed thighs, she was sending Rachel into ecstasy. Chloe's hands moved upwards to pinch and play with Rachel's nipples, while her mouth still played with her clit, exciting Rachel more and more.

"Would you like me to fuck you?"

"Yes please," begged Rachel.

Chloe reached for her bag, unzipped it and took out a gleaming white vibrator, which made Rachel shiver with anticipation. Chloe laid down beside her friend and switched on the vibrator. She began to run it up and down the inside of Rachel's thighs. Then slowly, she brushed it against her aching pussy, teasing the lips apart and pushing it inside. With the vibrator inside her Rachel was about to come, and she reached down to rub her clitoris harder and harder. "Fuck me Chloe . . fuck me. Let me see the vibrator going in and out of my pussy."

Chloe thrust the vibrator in and out, "Like this?" she said. "Do you want it like this?"

Chloe moved the vibrator faster than ever.

"Yes . . Yes," said Rachel. Her body convulsed and shuddered, and she cried out loudly as her orgasm swept through her.

As Rachel's orgasm subsided, Chloe took the vibrator from inside her. Pulling her own knickers to one side, she plunged it into her throbbing pussy. Her back arched as she thrust it in and out, and felt the rush of her own orgasm take control. Her body shook violently, and she writhed till the last waves of contented bliss washed over her. She threw back her head and sighed with the release of so much pent up sexual tension.

They lay together on the bed, side by side, gently kissing each other, giggling like schoolgirls at their naughtiness.

"Let's have a coffee and then go out somewhere," suggested Chloe.

As Rachel sipped her coffee, she watched Chloe across the table. She tingled as she thought of what they had done. This day had not turned out the way she had expected. The laundry was still there, the sink was still full of sticky plates, and the ironing hadn't been touched. But all Rachel could think of was Chloe, and what they would do tomorrow.

Bettina writes,

While I was staying with my brother in Canada, I needed to be able to receive e-mails from my publisher in England. My brother is a lawyer, and he said I could have them sent to his office. When I got there, his secretary Emma was at lunch so I was able to use her computer. I clicked on the 'Get Mail' icon, and on to the screen came the following two e-mails. I read them, and could not resist printing them out for myself. Just as I was hoping not to get caught, in walked Emma. She asked me who I was and what I was doing. I had to own up, but she was the one who was blushing.

The E-mail

THE E-MAIL

To: Emma@xxxxx. xxx
message :

> > Dear Emma,

I thought it was time to write to you about my new guy. He is great and I wish you could meet him. He is kind and generous, and has a great sense of humour. He's tall, with dark wavy hair, and deep blue eyes which are really sexy. He has a smouldering smile that makes my tocs curl. His name is Simon, and I met him at the club, remember, the one where you met Mike.

Simon's very romantic, and he's teaching me so much about life. Mind you, he is a bit older than me, but that just means he knows so much more than I do - about everything. We have been together for nearly two months now, and we see each other every weekend. The thing I'm into at the moment, is sex in the shower. It's my favourite, and it's such a turn on. The feel of the warm water on my skin, our bodies touching, the sensation of liquid running over my pussy - it's so delicious. It was a glorious thing to discover and I'm really glad that Simon enjoys it as much as I do. Anyway, let me tell you about the first time, and promise me you'll give it a try. Mike will love it.

We'd been out for the evening at the local, and to be honest we'd had rather too much to drink, so Simon asked me to stay over. I didn't want to drive home as I was well over the limit. He has a big flat near Cedar Road, and I love staying there, because apart from being able to sleep with Simon, it's so much nicer than my pokey little bed-sit. When we have sex at my place, we have to be quiet, as so many people can hear us. I only have to sigh, for someone to knock on the wall. At Simon's flat we have a bathroom and kitchen all to ourselves, as well as his bed-room, and a huge living room. We aren't confined to the bed, we can do it wherever we like. Nobody can hear us so I can be as loud as I want. You know how loud I am, from when we used to share the flat. Remember when Jake stayed over at Christmas that time, and no one could get any sleep because of the noise that was coming from my room. And at breakfast Tom was calling me the 'cum queen'!

Anyway, back to what I was telling you. Simon made me a drink and asked me if I wanted to take a shower. I took my glass into the bathroom, and Simon followed with a large soft towel, which he draped over the radiator. Then, he put down the loo seat and sat on the lid. He watched as I removed my clothes. I had on that red dress, you know, the one I love. I stepped into the shower. The water was warm and ran in rivulets down my face and between my breasts. The lather from the soap felt luxurious as I massaged it over my tummy and between my legs. As I concentrated on keeping the water in the shower tray, I felt Simon's hand caress my back. He took the soap from me, and began to tenderly soap my back. The feeling of his touch on my skin made my nipples pert and sensitive. I longed for his hand to brush against them.

Taking the initiative for once, I turned to face him and unbuckled the belt of his trousers. His cock was straining for release, and my hand lingered over it as I pulled down his zip. I slipped his trousers over his hips revealing his magnificent erection. I tugged his boxer shorts over it and let them fall to the floor. He unbuttoned his shirt, and I took it from his strong arms, leaving him naked in front of me. He pushed me against the tiles and pressed his body against mine. His huge cock pushed into my stomach, and I could feel my pussy beginning to throb. I let out a sigh as he slid his hand between my legs, and his fingers searched for my clit. He dipped a finger inside me and rubbed my juices all over my pussy, as I eagerly pushed my hips towards his hand. He sank to his knees, and buried his head between my thighs, licking at the wetness inside with his tongue. I opened my legs wider to give him more room, and he played roughly with my breasts as wonderful feelings shot through my body. He dragged me on to the shower tray and took the shower head in his hand. He sprayed the warm jet of water directly on to my clitoris, and then he turned the controls, so that cold jets of water shot into my pussy making me squirm. The feelings were so intense, like no others I had ever experienced before . . . . it was bliss. The water trickled down my pussy and teased my clit till I was beside myself with pleasure. Then he pushed his enormous cock into my mouth. He pushed forward and back, his penis slipping in, and then nearly out of my mouth as I sucked on it. He kept going, and it felt good. I held the base of it to give me some control. This seemed to excite him more and he got faster. As his cock thrust into my mouth, I could feel it twitch against my tongue. His hands were gripping my hair, and he pulled it tighter, his fingers curling round the roots. I usually pull my mouth away when I know my man is about to come, but this time I was so hot and excited that I wanted to keep going. His cock pulsated as cum shot into my mouth and throat. I swallowed it, it tasted good. I sucked at every last drop, though some oozed from my lips and was washed away by the shower.

We began to wash each other with soapy lather. As he touched me, I was still so aroused and wanted my own orgasm. He sucked my nipples, then he turned me around, and I leaned my hands on the cold white tiles in front of me, so that my back arched and my arse stuck out. His hand slid up my thigh and into my wide open pussy. I knew that I was about to come so I pushed his hand away. I wanted sex.

I took the shower head and playfully sprayed Simon. I took his penis in my hand, and turned the shower spray on to it, whilst I continued to arouse it with my hand. It soon became hard again and I wanted it deep inside me.

We stepped out of the shower, and I took the warm

towel and laid it on the bathroom floor. I knelt down on all fours and told Simon to fuck me hard. He knelt behind me, parted my legs and rubbed my clit. I could not bear any more of his teasing but had to have his cock inside me, fucking me. He pushed his cock deep inside my waiting pussy. He thrusted in and out, faster and faster, until I could feel myself coming. I reached a climax that went on and on. I must have made a lot of noise, because it was the best orgasm I'd ever had. Just as I'd finished, he withdrew from me, and ejaculated all over my arse. We both lay back with exhaustion. After a few minutes I got up to take a shower!

I'm so horny after writing this e-mail, I need a good fuck tonight - Simon's back in an hour so I'm going to turn the radiator on in the bathroom!

E-mail me back when you can, and tell me all about what you and Mike get up to. I want all the details.

Love & Kisses, Georgie.

P.S. Have you still got that double-headed dildo we had so much fun with - you naughty girl!

\> >
< < < < < < < < < < < < < < < < < < < < < < < < < < < < < <
reply :

> > Dear Georgie,

Thanks for your e-mail. No, I haven't got that dildo anymore, I thought you had it. Perhaps Sarah stole it, she was always nicking things of mine. She must be having some fun with it, wherever she's moved to. I always thought she was a bit of a closet dyke.

Your e-mail really made me hot, and when Mike came in, I was playing with myself, which made him horny as hell. We had great sex, and even tried it in the shower. It was OK, but our shower space isn't as big as yours, so it was a bit restricting. Mind you, we were so turned on by your antics that we got very excited, and our love-making lasted for ages.

I don't know if I should tell you what we enjoy most, as lots of people seem to find it disgusting. They should be more open minded, as it makes sex brilliant - but whatever turns you on. Don't be put off. . . we like anal sex. You should try it just once, in case you don't know what you're missing. If you do it gently, it shouldn't hurt at all. I'll tell you what we do, then maybe you will want to try it for yourself.

The first time we had anal sex it scared me a bit, but Mike promised that he wouldn't hurt me, and I trust him with all my heart, so I was prepared to give it a go. We lay, tucked into each other, and Tony played with my pussy till it was soaking wet. I pushed my bottom towards him, and he softly began to rub my tight anus with my juices. I could feel myself become more and more aroused, and my pussy ached for him to go inside. His huge cock pressed against my back, and I played with him, making him groan out loud. I felt him spasm with pleasure as his straining erection grew behind me. Then I felt his fingers open my anus, and gently probe inside. To my surprise, I found it incredibly exciting, and muscles contracted tightly around his fingers. I remember wondering how on earth would I be able to accept his manhood into such a small hole, but I knew he wouldn't hurt me. His fingers widened my anus, and he moved down my body, ready to push the tip of his cock into my expectant hole. Then he reached under the bed for a tube of jelly, and smoothed it on to his erection, sighing as he stroked it's length. Taking a blob of cold jelly, he rubbed it into the entrance of my anus, and pushed his finger deep inside me as I writhed with pleasure. Then, opening my hole a little more, he used the jelly to push in another finger. He played it around the edges of my hole. When he felt I was ready, he gently probed the entrance with his cock, and I was amazed to find that it felt wonderful. I pulled him nearer to me, pushing his thick erection deep inside. I couldn't believe how good it felt, pulsing strongly inside my anus. As he fucked me harder and harder, my muscles gripped his cock so much tighter than my cunt ever could. Then I felt him explode deep inside me, and as his warm cum shot into my body, he shook violently next to me, and held on until his orgasm gently subsided.

Just as gently, he withdrew from me, and his fingers probed my cunt, delicately searching for my clit. He circled it round and round until I came. My body arched, as the feelings of climax pulsed through me. I came in one of the most explosive orgasms I have ever had.

I had not expected anal sex to be so good, but it was one of the most wonderful sexual experiences Mike has ever given me.

Ask Simon if he fancies doing it that way. E-mail me soon and let me know whether you give it a try, and tell me what you think.

Good screwing,

much love and kisses, Emma.

Bettina writes,

I recently received the following account of a train journey. But before I comment on it, I'll let you read on . . .

Underground

UNDERGROUND

Rob knew he had to rush if he was to catch the last train home. He ran down the passage towards the steps, feeling that rush of air that signalled the imminent arrival of a train. As he got to the top of the stairs, he saw the train enter the station, emerging from the darkness of the tunnel at the end of the platform. Jumping down two steps at a time, he thought he might slip, but he managed to land safely just as the doors whooshed open. Looking around, he realised that he was the only passenger catching the train. As he stepped on to the train, he noticed that the carriages were not entirely empty. He was glad that he wasn't alone as this made him feel somehow safer. It didn't seem to matter these days whether you were male or female, it was wise to take care. Only last week he had read about a man being raped, although he couldn't quite work out how. Anyway, he wasn't alone, so it didn't much matter. He glanced around at the other passengers in his carriage, and was careful not to sit directly next to anybody. He brushed the seat he had chosen, and placing his ruck sack and jacket in the vacant place next to his own, sat down.

Fidgeting slightly to get more comfortable, he moved on to one hip and crossed his long slim legs. Looking around for the second time, he began to notice his companions. To his left were a young couple who seemed very engrossed in each other. They were whispering and kissing, and the young man's hand played shyly with his boyfriend's hair. Rob looked away, perturbed. He had nothing against gays, but watching public affection between two men made him feel slightly uneasy. He cast his gaze further up the carriage, only to be met by the stony stare of an old woman. She seemed to have her entire world packed inside two very large bags. She was wearing at least two overcoats, the top one looking very shabby, and a pair of mens boots that had definitely seen better days. In her hand she held a three-quarters full bottle, of what he presumed to be spirits. As their eyes met, he knew that he had committed the cardinal sin of staring. He thought, that knowing his luck, she would probably come over to hurl some abuse at him. So, it was a great relief when the train pulled into the next station, and she shuffled out, muttering as she went. The young men got up and left too, the doors closed, and the train shuddered back to it's steady rhythm.

Walking towards him down the carriage was a young woman, who, to his surprise, came and sat directly opposite him. He looked into her face, and was surprised to find her brown eyes staring straight back at his. Rob smiled shyly, and she smiled right back. Trying to be casual, he dropped his gaze, and let his eyes wander slowly up to her face again. Her mouth was slightly open, and she softly licked her top lip with the tip of her tongue. She smiled some more. Rob was stunned. She was teasing him. He watched as she put her index finger to her lips, sucked it for a moment, and then seductively drew it down her neck, slipping it inside her silky blouse. Rob squirmed in his seat, feeling embarrassed, but turned on, both at the same time. He felt his neck getting hotter and hotter.

From watching her hand gently rub the flesh under her blouse, he looked down to her legs, which slowly slid apart on the polished train floor as his eyes fell on them. It was as if his eyes were activating her movements, first her smile and teasing tongue, then her hand inside her blouse, and now her legs opening, all answering his unspoken requests. Her skirt seemed to have rubbed itself all the way to the top of her legs. White flesh separated it from the stockings tops. Between her legs was a neat black triangle. He focused his attention on it, hoping she would respond as she had before. She began to open her legs a little more, and her fingers slid down to her pussy. As he watched, her fingers began to slip inside the lips. Rob moved his hands on to his lap to cover his fly, which was straining against his bulging erection. He gazed in awe at her beautiful pussy, displayed for only him. He glanced up to her blouse, where her other hand undid the buttons, and revealed her soft white breasts. She took her wet finger from between her legs, and used it to massage her nipples, till they were hard. She slid forward, exposing more of her delicately reddening pussy, and bent her knee to bring her stiletto heeled shoe up to her plump buttock.

She slipped off the shoe, and sighing breathlessly, she

began to rub her clitoris with the long, thin, hard heel. Rubbing the heel up and down, she pressed her body further into the prickly seat. Her head moved backwards in delight, and her free hand slid under her raised leg to insert a finger into her warm inviting hole. Rob wanted to push his cock into it, to feel it's tight grip. He rubbed his hand up and down his fly, the warm denim under his fingers giving friction against his hard shaft.

Entranced, he watched as the girl writhed before him, spasms and judders of climax pulsing through her young body. At the final peak of her orgasm, the lights of the carriage flickered out. He felt her kiss his lips gently and sensuously, and he opened his mouth to take in more of her lips and tongue, but she drew away. When the lights flickered back on, she was gone.

He stood and looked around but she had disappeared. On her seat lay a card which Rob picked up and put in his inside pocket.

It read:

BETTINA VARESE
The Queen of Tease

Bettina writes,

Well Reader, can you imagine me doing something like that?

Bettina writes,

Late last year, in the Orion Club, I found a handbag hanging on the back of a toilet door. I just had to look in it, because I could see the tip of a vibrator poking out of the top. Inside was a spare battery, some make-up, sachets of perfume, tissues, condoms and a small black diary.

Now, I know it's bad manners to read someone's diary, but I couldn't resist peeking inside. After reading some of it, I really wanted to meet this girl. The barman said he knew who the bag belonged to, so I hung around at the bar. When she came to collect it, she thanked me and bought me a drink. We chatted and I told her I was a writer. I said her diary had got me all hot and turned on, and that as I collect erotica, I wanted to have a copy of it. When she realised I wasn't joking, she was really into the idea. Here's an extract from it. If you like it, write and tell me, so I can put some more of it in future books.

Diary of a Nympho

DIARY OF A NYMPHO

Sun:

Had a late night last night at the Orion Club, but boy oh boy the sex was good. Wore my newest, shortest skirt, and the smallest top I could find. I made sure that my tits looked really pert to attract the guys. Could hardly walk in my stilettos. Had to remember to be very ladylike as I wasn't wearing any panties. Well, I wanted to Sharon Stone anyone I really fancied.

There was this Caribbean guy there, and by the cut of his trousers he was hung like a horse. I made a play for him and got lucky. He shagged me senseless in the alley behind the club. He was brilliant, and went at it like a stallion. His cock was massive. He made me suck him off, and I couldn't take him all in my mouth. When he came, I couldn't swallow it all as there was too much, and it went all down my chin and over my boobs.

My pussy was sore afterwards, so when the cabbie on the way home asked me for a quickie instead of his fare, I just had to refuse. This surprised him, as usually I'm up for it. But then I felt sorry for him, and as I didn't have any money on me anyway, I gave him a hand job. It didn't take long, and now I have two lots of stains to wash out of my clothes!

Mon:

Had the most amazing bit of luck today at lunchtime. I was feeling as randy as hell this morning. I gave myself a good fingering in the toilets at work, but that didn't do the trick. It just gave me a stitch, as it wasn't a very comfortable position. Anyway, I went out at lunchtime to get a sandwich, and I bumped in to Phil. He is always a randy old sod. He didn't disappoint me and asked me back to his flat to eat - but it wasn't a snack he had in mind. I'd only just sat down, when he dropped to the floor, pulled off my panties, and pushed my legs apart so that he could give me a good licking. God his tongue felt ace. He sucked me dry, and I gave his cock a really good seeing to. I love eating cock and his fits my mouth so well. It's divine letting my tongue lick up and down his throbbing prick, tasting his salty cum as it oozes from the tip. I love to tease him, and right when he can't take anymore, I like to sit on his huge erection, and ride him till I feel him explode inside me. He knows exactly what to do with his fingers, and he can always make me orgasm. Mind you, it was only lunch break so we didn't have long. I just had time to clean myself up before going back to work, and boy was I starving all afternoon. He asked me back for lunch tomorrow but we'll have to see.

Anyway, I thought I'd had all the luck for one day, but things got better. I got home at the normal time to find this really hunky guy moving into the flat downstairs. He obviously worked out, as his body looked really toned and his shoulders were broad. So I decided to play 'Little

Girl Lost' and pretended I had locked myself out. He fell for that old gag, hook, line and sinker, and it was only a matter of minutes before I was inside his flat. I turned on the tears and played dizzy, but I didn't have to try too hard as I could see him eyeing me up when he thought I was crying. He came over to where I was sitting and put his arm round me, giving it the old TLC. When his face got close enough, I kissed him full on the lips, and stuck my tongue in his mouth. Typical male, I could feel his cock rise to the bait, so it wasn't very hard getting him to fuck the living daylights out of me. He stood me in front of him and one by one he undid the buttons on my dress which fell to the floor. Then he pulled my panties down and sank his head into my cunt. What bliss! He even admired the fact that I'd shaved my pussy. He said it made his job so much easier, and as I opened my legs, I felt his tongue searching my already soaking wet pussy and his hands massaged my bottom, playing with the crack of my arse, which was such a turn on. Then he stripped off his clothes, and I saw his enormous cock bounce to attention as he pulled off his underpants. Don't blokes look fucking stupid standing there in shoes and socks. I could smell the scent of him and took him into my mouth as deep as I could, licking at it as he groaned with pleasure. He was a bit rough when he pushed me to the floor and plunged his huge cock into my tight pussy. His roughness turned me on even more. His hips arched in time to my cunt as he thrust himself in and out of me. After one almighty sigh I felt his warm cum shoot into me as he shuddered and orgasmed. But I was not disappointed by his quickie fuck, because when he withdrew he pushed my legs wide apart and sucked on my clit with his hot hungry mouth until I came. It was so intense I had to push him away in case I pissed all over him. Writing this down has made me feel really horny, so I'll finish now and play with my vibrator. Oooh.

Tues:
My fanny hurts from all the pleasure I got last night with my new vibrator. I got it from one of those women-only sex parties. They are such a laugh. At the last one I went to we played silly games with condoms that tasted of different fruits, and an aerosol of whipped cream. I don't know who kept the photos, but they must be pretty embarrassing.

Couldn't believe what happened today. I was playing with myself, and thinking dirty thoughts, when I suddenly realised that someone was watching me. Some little pervert had made a hole in the cubicle wall of the toilets at work, and I could see this eye looking through it. I didn't have a clue who it was, but I thought I'll give the dirty bugger something to watch, so I stuck my hand inside my top and exposed my tits. I squeezed them and pushed them together, massaging them and then pinching my nipples between my fingers and thumb. Then, pretending I hadn't seen his peep-hole at all, I gave myself a really good fingering, licking my juices from my fingers and sinking them deep inside my pussy, the whole works. I could feel the cubicles rock as whoever it was wanked themselves off.

Funnily enough, it made me feel really randy and I needed a good screw. So, when I went out tonight and got that cabbie again, I thought I'd let him fuck me. But, he said as I only gave him a hand job last time, I'd have to make up for it by giving him some breast relief first. As my tits are 36DD, he knew he was in for a good time. But, I never got the fuck I wanted as the stupid sod came between my breasts as soon as he had begun. It went all over my tits and my face. I tried to get his cock up again but the tosser was spent. What a wanker.

Wed:
I can't believe it but yesterdays perv turned out to be Stuart from accounts! I've fancied him for ages. I went in the loo around the same time, and there was the eye peeping through that hole again. I thought I'd give him what he wanted, so I got my vibrator out of my bag and started playing with it. I began by circling it round and round my clit, then I pushed it into my cunt right in front of the peep-hole. I turned around to let him see my pussy from behind with my legs apart. I reached my hand round behind my arse and inserted the vibrator inside me while I gasped and moaned. Then I thought, what the hell, let's go and see who this creep is. I pulled up my knickers and dived into the gents next door. There, bending over with his face pressed up against the cubicle wall, was Stuart. I was shocked it was him, but really glad because I'd wanted

to shag him for months. He had always seemed so quiet, never flirting with everyone like the rest of us. Still, it's always the quiet ones isn't it? Knowing his dirty little secret had been found out, his face went bright red. I said if he didn't shag me right there and then, I was going to tell everyone what he'd been up to. I told him to unzip his trousers and get his prick out. It was of no use to me in that condition, so I played with it for what seemed like an eternity and it finally got hard. I pulled my knickers down, turned round and placed my hands on the back wall of the cubicle, spreading my legs so that he could take me from behind. I felt his stiff cock pushing tentatively up against my pussy lips, and I said to him, "Fucking hell Stuart, what d'you need a written invitation?" I put my hand behind me to grab his cock and get it inside me. Then pushing against the wall, I started to move backwards and forwards on to it. As my tight pussy closed around his cock and slid up and down it's length, I noticed that the hole in the wall was right in front of me. I looked through it. Karen was in there having a pee. My handbag was still hanging on the door of the cubicle, and sticking out of the top of it was my vibrator.

Karen took it out and looked at it, switching it on and off. I was amazed to see her begin to rub herself with the tip of the vibrator. She is always such a sweet and innocent little thing. She slid it up her inner thigh and when it reached her clit, she moved it around, slipping it in and out of her cunt. Her cheeks flushed and she got really turned on. My own pussy was throbbing so hot with the sight of her, and I started to tell Stuart what I could see. I described Karen, her blonde hair and blue eyes, her long smooth legs and tight outfit, and her breasts squeezed in to a little white blouse. I told Stuart what she was doing with the vibrator to her open wet pussy. With every word he thrusted harder and harder, he was really getting off on it. Now he was hard as a fucking rock. He shafted me faster and faster. As my climax began, I could feel his pulsating cock spurting cum deep inside me, and at that same moment Karen cried out with the pleasure she was giving to herself, the vibrator deep inside her. My body filled with a tingling, explosive orgasm, as the last of Stuart's cum shot into me. Then Karen must have heard us, as she hurriedly picked herself up and fled the toilets.

When I went back to the office, Karen was busy at the typewriter. I gave her a knowing smile as I sat at my desk opposite her's. I thought I'd probably leave a damp patch on my seat at the end of day, because all I could think about was what I saw her doing at lunchtime. God knows what state my knickers were in by five o'clock. I was beginning to think I was turning into a perv like Stuart.

When I got home I had a shower before Craig came round. He has no idea what I get up to. If he did he'd be well pissed off.

Thurs:
Today started well, but by mid-morning I was in the fucking shit. First thing I had a shower, and was trying to dress when the bell went. So, slipping on my dressing gown for

the sake of decency, I opened the door to find Kevin the milkman there, waiting for his money. Of course I invited him in, letting the gown slip open, tantalising him with a bit of nipple. I knew he couldn't resist, so it was only a matter of minutes before we were on the floor fucking wildly. There wasn't enough time for pissing about, so I just opened my legs and he unzipped his fly. His cock was ready for action. Thank God for milkman, they walk around with a constant hard-on. They *always* deliver. In no time he was giving it his all, thrusting his more than generous dick deep into my well lubricated cunt. We panted all the way to our climax as I felt his hot spunk shoot into me. He sucked greedily at my tits as his orgasm pulsed through his body. Then calmly, as though nothing had happened, he got up and zipped up his trousers. Apologizing profusely, he left, saying there would be no charge for my milk that week.

This meant I had to have another shower, missed my bus and was late for work. Mr. Trimble was not pleased. As soon as I got to work he called me into his office. He's about fifty, been in the same job all his working life, and has worked his way up to the grand position of 'supervisor'. He's a slimy little git and he's always trying to touch me up. He said, now that I had been warned three times about being late, he was going to have to sack me. But, he said, there was something I could do to change his mind. With that, Slimy Git locked the door, undid his trousers and sat in his chair behind the desk. I told him that no way was I going to suck him off. He said if I didn't, I'd lose my job for sure. Then I thought to myself well, what's five minutes, I could never find another job this easy and make such good money. I knelt down and there was his penis staring me in the face. I closed my eyes and took it in my mouth. It smelt of stale urine and I felt like gagging. I gripped the base with my hand to try to hurry things along. He was pushing my head down further on to his dick. Suddenly I felt a dribble of spunk fall on to my tongue. It was all over. It wouldn't fill a fucking thimble. What a fucking wanker.

I couldn't get the taste out of my mouth, so after work I went to the pub, got pissed, went home, crashed out.

Fri:

Best day of the week. I got up thinking about the club tonight. I know I'd have to get there early if I was going to get my hands on Jules before Dee pulled him. She's a right old slapper. I made sure I got to work on time.

Karen and I were sent to do some photocopying in the utilities room. We were in there by ourselves, and the copier was churning out piles of paper. It's always so warm in there with all the machinery. As usual the conversation was boyfriends and sex. Karen was telling me how much she likes it when her boyfriend French kisses her. She's so inexperienced for seventeen years old, I'd done everything by then. I said to her that I'd got a really good technique for French kissing and that I could show her if she liked. I kissed her and my tongue pushed it's way between her lips into her mouth. At first she pulled away from me, but then she got into it and her tongue became just as eager as mine. I hitched up her skirt and I pushed my hand up between her legs. Her knickers were damp. I slid my hand inside them and found her clit. It was small but became hard under my fingers. I was driving her wild and she was loving every minute. I rubbed her clit and then teased her hot pussy with light fingertips. It didn't take long before I brought her to orgasm. She came, and I had to put my hand over her mouth to stop her from making too much noise or we would have been discovered. The photocopier had finished. We quickly picked up our stuff and put our clothes straight again. We went back to our desks for a tedious two hours.

I was really horny all afternoon and by the time I got to the club I was desperate for a shag. I wore my favourite zip-up, 'fuck-me' dress, with hold-up stockings, black lace knickers and no bra. I got there really early and they weren't open yet, but the barman Jules let me in. It was just me and him and two of the Orion bouncers. I knew Jules was a really good fuck because I got off with him a few weeks ago. The two bouncers were a bit tasty too, so I didn't know who to flirt with first. They said they were having drinks in a back room and I could join them if I fancied it. I followed them into a dimly lit room. Once inside the door, one of the bouncers turned the key and locked us in. Then the fun began. First they pulled off my clothes. Then they took it in turns to play with my tits which were red hot with excitement. Then one after another they made me give them blow jobs, as the others played with my cunt, making me wetter than I'd ever been before. Jules opened my legs and the other two each took an ankle as his head sank into my pussy. I felt his tongue licking in and out of my swollen cunt. I arched my back as his tongue probed my lips for my clit, and his hands rubbed my nipples. Then one of the bouncers sat across my chest, and pushed his prick into my mouth so that I could barely breathe. I sucked at it until he could obviously take no more, because he swapped with his friend and I found a new cock pushing it's way into my mouth. All the time Jules sucked on my clit and I was so fucking excited I thought I was going to come. I could taste a salty bead of spunk on the very end of the cock and I sucked harder, making the guy groan and gasp with pleasure. Then he withdrew it from my mouth.

Jules pulled his head from my pussy and told me to kneel on all fours. I felt a thrill of anticipation of what they would do to me next. I began to experience delicious sex. I felt fingers that were moist search my cunt until I nearly came. One bouncer knelt behind me and pushed his huge, hard prick in to my waiting pussy. Fuck, it was big. It slid in and out of me while his hands pressed down on my arse. Jules came round to my face and put his cock into my mouth. It was such an amazing turn-on to have a cock in my mouth and a cock in my cunt at the same time. Both of them fucking me at once. I felt my orgasm building up and I had the most incredible climax I have ever had, while they both went for it at the same time, harder into my cunt and faster into my mouth. They both shot their cum into me, exploding into my cunt, shooting into my throat and overflowing out of my mouth. God it was incredible. Of course the other bouncer hadn't finished his fun yet, so he turned me over and fucked me till he came as well.

I hope there was video tape in the security cameras, if so, I'm gonna be the star of the club!

Writing this down has got me all horny again as usual but I have to go to sleep now - I'm all shagged out.

Bettina writes,

The story coming up is, 'Bonding'. It was given to me by a girlfriend, who dated the guy called James, who you will see is telling the story. He swore it was all true.

Bonding

BONDING

I first saw her in the club, when I was with some mates. She was standing by the bar, sipping at her drink, and looking casually around as though she was waiting for someone. Our eyes met for a moment, but then I was distracted by the arrival of my best mate Cal, who slapped me on the back and offered to buy me a pint. When I looked again, she was walking towards the ladies with another girl. I returned my attention to Cal and forgot all about her.

The next time I saw her was on the way to the pub one evening. As we passed each other, she acknowledged me briefly, and then continued to walk by.

So, when I spotted her waiting at the bus stop with some carrier bags, and it had just begun to rain, I knew I had the opportunity to get to know her better. When I say better, I certainly could not have predicted the things I was about to discover.

Let me say at this point, that I'm a regular kind of guy. I'm not particularly handsome, but I'm not ugly either. I'm tall and fair, have well developed muscles, and can usually find the kind of women that attract me. I'd been pretty unlucky recently though, so there seemed no harm in trying it on. I stopped the car, opened the window, and called out to her. She didn't hesitate for a second. She came straight over to me, and I offered her a lift home. I was taken aback when she grabbed her shopping and jumped straight in beside me.

I couldn't help looking at her as I drove. Her skirt, which was extremely short, rode even further up her beautiful slim, slender legs. Don't get me wrong, I'm no kind of pervert, but you just can't help noticing things like that. I tried to concentrate on my driving, and asked her a few questions about herself. She was quite forthright, and seemed very chatty. In fact, I could hardly get a word in edgeways. But talking isn't one of my strong points, so I just let her get on with it.

Before long, I knew her name, age, address and place of work, as well as a potted family history. Typical of a woman, can't stop once they've started. But it hardly mattered because I wasn't thinking about long term relationships. She said her name was Mandy, and I wanted to reply, "Fly me," but somehow I thought she might be too young to understand, or offended by my remark. So I told her my name was James, and then I shut up. I'd got too far to mess it up now, and I didn't want to ruin my chances.

I pulled the car up outside the address she had given me, and waited to see what she would do. She climbed out of the car and put her bags on the pavement. "Shit," I thought to myself, she isn't going to ask me in. I was wrong. She turned, leaned back into the car, and said "Coming in?"

I couldn't get out of the car quick enough. As I fumbled

for my keys to lock up the car, she was bending over sorting out her shopping bags. Her thighs were slightly apart, and her skirt slipped slowly upwards. At the very top of her legs, her tight, white panties slipped into the crease of her arse. Man I thought I'd died and gone to heaven. All kind of thoughts were whizzing through my head. So far things were going like a dream and I didn't want to wake up. This kind of thing only happens to other people.

Like a lost sheep I followed her through a door. She turned a light on in the hall and climbed a flight of stairs, with me following eagerly behind. She reached her front door, and took out a key from her jacket pocket, which let us into a flat. She dropped her bags in the hallway and called out, "Sam I'm back." My heart sank - she's married and I'm an idiot. So, you can imagine my relief when another young girl walked out from one of the rooms. She was equally attractive, and had soft, shoulder length, auburn hair. Mandy disappeared into the bathroom.

The new girl smiled as she took me by the hand and led me back into the room she had come from. It seemed an intimate thing to do to a stranger. She showed me to a plush thirties style sofa, the type that Gloria Grahame had sunk back into in those old black and white movies. I took the drink she offered me. Her eyes looked into mine constantly as we chatted. When I spoke, she sucked at a cherry on a cocktail stick. The cherry disappeared between her lips for an instant, and emerged glistening and shiny. She took it from the stick and pushed it into my mouth. I couldn't believe my luck, Sam wanted me. If I had read

Mandy's signals right, I was going to have a problem choosing between them. Little did I know what they had planned, although if I had, I would certainly have wanted to stay exactly where I was.

Sam leaned forward and kissed me. She began to lightly caress my legs. It felt good. She continued even as Mandy entered the room. I felt uneasy. It seemed my choice had been made for me.

Sam left me, and went over to join Mandy. I drank slowly, taking gulps of the sweet alcohol in the glass. I was beginning to feel very relaxed. I was trying to listen to what they were saying, but I couldn't make it out. I remember thinking that the drink might have had something in it, but to be honest I didn't really care. I watched them talk. Sam was wearing almost the same outfit as Mandy. Both wore short, light coloured skirts and tight fitting tops. Both had bare legs and high sling back shoes. As they talked, Mandy started to touch Sam. She stroked her shoulders, and then her breasts. I couldn't believe my eyes. I figured this was all done for my benefit, so I settled back to enjoy the show. She lifted Sam's skirt, and slipped her hand over the panties and between her legs. As the fingers moved around, Sam rolled her head backwards, sighing with pleasure.

"Look at Sam's arse, isn't it beautiful James?"

"Yes," I replied, trying not to sound too eager. Mandy led Sam over to me, prompting her to kneel in front of me. Mandy went behind me, and I felt her long, sexy arms weave themselves around my neck, and her large breasts push into my shoulder. Her hands slid into the neck of my shirt and wandered seductively down my chest, stopping at my nipples, where she began to rub teasingly. Then, as they hardened and became sensitive, she pulled away and ran her warm hands down further, until she reached the buckle of my trousers. I realised that I was no longer in control of the situation, and that Mandy had taken the lead role in a delicious game. The two of them giggled and whispered to each other. Mandy undid my trousers, and Sam pulled them down as I obligingly lifted my hips from the chair. I felt a bit vulnerable in this state, but I was too excited to object. Sam untied my shoelaces, removed my shoes and socks, and then pulled my trousers from my ankles. Mandy unbuttoned my shirt, and I dropped it to the floor. This was better than I had dared to hope. Two beautiful girls who both wanted me, and at the same time too.

Mandy told me to stand up. Both girls took my hands and led me into a bedroom. They told me to lie down on the iron bed. The crisp, white sheets were cold to the touch. My boxer shorts strained with the erection underneath. Sam pulled them from me and threw them to one side. My penis stood erect, and I must say, I was quite proud at that moment. Mandy opened a drawer and took out two scarves, which she used to tie my hands to the bed posts. She tied them very tightly, and I had to beg her to loosen them a bit. Sam leaned over the bed, and from beneath it pulled out what looked like a broomstick. To be honest, I did flinch a little then, as I wasn't quite sure what they had in mind, although strung up as I was it was a bit late to argue. Sam handed it across to Mandy, who started to tie my legs to it, as wide apart as she could, using two more scarves. I realised that they were practised in the art of seduction, and wondered how many other men had fallen for their charms. But the girls didn't leave me time to think that one through, and they began to remove each others clothes.

Mandy unbuttoned Sam's top. Underneath was a black, lacy bra, which tightly encased her small, shapely breasts. Mandy reached round to unclip the bra, and tossed it on the floor. She squeezed Sam's breasts, and gently fondled her dark pink nipples. As she removed the rest of Sam's clothes, I wanted to touch the slightly rounded belly, and soft triangle of shaped pussy hair. Her legs were long and shapely, and I begged to be untied so that I could touch both of their beautiful bodies. Both girls sssh'd me.

Sam, in one motion, pulled Mandy's skirt and panties down to the floor, and then lifted her top, peeling it off over her head, revealing her bare breasts. They were firm, but much larger than Sam's. I saw at once that she had completely shaved her pussy, which made her seem child-like, although she didn't behave like any child I'd ever met. Her sexuality just oozed from every pore, and I could smell her sweet scent from where I lay. Mandy climbed on to the bed. She lay next to me, letting her large breasts fall upon my cock, which by now was near bursting. It seemed to have a life of it's own, as her skin brushed against it. She rubbed her long fingers over my nipples which hardened with excitement. Then, Sam climbed on to the other side of the bed, and sandwiched my body between her's and Mandy's. But instead of touching my body, she leaned her small breasts against my chest, and began to touch Mandy, who responded with little gasps of delight. Her small fingers played gently up and down Mandy's soft neck and chest, occasionally touching those wonderful breasts which quivered onto me. This just aroused me further.

Leaning over me with her back arched, her arse in the air, and her legs parted, Sam placed her mouth over my erect penis. Mandy placed her hands on Sam's bum, parting her cheeks with her fingertips, and letting her tongue lick softly at the open lips of the wet pussy. I ached to be able to do the same, and begged, in vain, to be released. I was dying to sink my cock into either cunt and fuck them, but the girls had other ideas.

Sam sucked on my cock, flicking her tongue back and forth, and taking all of me inside her mouth. Holding the base of it, she let her teeth bite lightly into the fragile hardness of my erection. All the time she moaned gently, as Mandy ate her sweet pussy juices. Sam began to stroke between my legs, and her fingers touched my anus. She took some of her love juice, and inserted a moist finger inside me, which made me writhe with pleasure. I pushed myself towards her to try to make her go deeper, but she withdrew her finger. She turned her attentions to Mandy, who took her beautiful face from Sam's bush and climbed on to my chest. She straddled me, facing the end of the bed, and pushed her warm and wet pussy up to my mouth. She sighed with delight, as I sunk my face between her thighs, sucking her, letting my tongue dart in and out, savouring those juices that flowed freely from her. She really enjoyed it as I sucked her, and she gasped and sighed with pleasure. She leaned forward so that she could kiss Sam, and play with her little breasts. They kissed deeply, tasting each others lips. I watched Mandy's pussy as it moved away from my face and hovered in front of me, as she attended to her love play with Sam. I wanted to fuck her so bad, my penis was burning, and so hard. As she sat back on to my face, Sam climbed on to my throbbing erection. She rose and fell, slipping her tight little pussy up and down my cock. I tried to stop myself from coming, because I wanted this to go on forever.

Just as I thought I could bear it no longer, she pulled away and climbed off me, allowing Mandy to take her place. I wanted to reach out for those beautiful breasts, as Mandy rode on my cock. From the side of the bed, Sam leaned forward over me, her moist juices just out of my tongue's reach. She began to suck on Mandy's hard nipples. She wrapped her arms around Mandy, so that she could play with my balls. I couldn't believe the sensations that shot through my body; this was like no other sex I'd ever experienced. I was in another world. Sam moved her sex closer to my face, so that my tongue could reach her sweet scent. It snaked into her tight, hot hole, drinking up her gorgeous juice. Mandy turned herself round, so that her back was tight up against Sam's breasts, allowing Sam to hold on tight to those beautiful large swollen nipples. As Mandy began to lift her hips faster and faster, Sam echoed the movement on my face, pushing herself into my mouth. Then Mandy pulled away from Sam's grasp, and still moving up and down on my erection, leaned forward and slid both hands between my legs. One hand curled around my balls, which tightened at the feel of her touch. Her other hand went further down, till her fingers touched lightly at my clenched anus. She turned her head towards me, and licked her middle finger seductively. As she plunged it deep into my tight hole, I couldn't hold back any longer. Sensations exploded through my body, and as she rode harder and harder on my cock, cum shot into her dripping wet cunt. Faster she rode on me, up and down, my penis pulsating inside her. Muscles rippled round her finger, and as she pulled it gently from me, I felt her orgasm over and over again. She cried out, "Yes . . yes . . fuck me." She screamed with the pleasure of my cock deep inside her.

Hardly waiting for these volcanic feelings to stop, she pulled Sam from my mouth, and spread her legs apart. Mandy fingered the pussy that glistened with droplets of juices, gently finding her hardened clit, which she played with, rubbing more and more. Backwards and forwards Sam pushed herself against the fingers that pleasured her. "Harder, harder," she cried. "Oh God, I'm coming. Oh, oh, God!" Sam's moans signalled her explosive orgasm.

She lay down beside me, and both girls stroked, and fondled each other, until their feelings of passion finally drifted away.

I lay there still spreadeagled on the bed, while they searched their wardrobe for new outfits to wear. After they'd dressed, Mandy finally untied me. I gave them my phone number, and they said they would ring me. I left, my head reeling, and I couldn't wait to tell Cal everything that had happened to me.

A month went by and I didn't hear anything from them. I returned to the flat and knocked on the door, only to find new tenants who had been there a couple of weeks.

Bettina writes,

A few months ago I did some modelling for a photographer friend of mine. His name is Rick, and we get on really well. The shots were for an exhibition he was having in London.

During the session he began to tell me about something that had recently happened to him. I thought he was just making it up, to turn me on during the shoot. But afterwards, when I questioned it's authenticity, the make-up artist, Tricia, confirmed that it was all true.

The Photo Shoot

THE PHOTO SHOOT

If there's one thing I look for in a model, it's exhibitionism. So many girls seem promising, but once the camera is loaded and pointing at them, they become totally inhibited. Why can't they relax and let themselves go? It's not like I'm a leering, dirty old man, with no artistic integrity, who just wants to see women with their clothes off. I'm young and good looking, and I'm told I've got a friendly face. I've had my photographs published as book covers, and in magazines, so girls know I'm serious.

I'm always on the look out for girls who are pretty enough to model for me. But like I said before, it's not just about being pretty, they have to have something extra.

I decided to go down to the Vortex Club. My friend Julian said that it would be a good place to find pretty girls. He's always down there, but I don't go clubbing as a rule. I hate the smoke, I hate the posers, and I'm not much of a drinker. The night I went down there, I couldn't see Julian around, so I went to the bar and ordered a drink.

The club was quite dark, but coloured spotlights fell on the dance floor. This made the dancers look like they were performing in a show. As my eyes scanned the floor, I could see two girls dancing provocatively together. One was brunette, and the other blonde. I couldn't take my eyes off them, but I found myself looking at the brunette most of the time. She wasn't tall, I'd say she was around five foot six, but then you don't have to be tall to be a photographic model. The camera always lies. She wore a short, tight, white top with something written on the front, black PVC hot pants, and shiny black knee high boots. Her shoulder-length hair was thick and tousled. She really looked like she was having a good time with her blonde friend.

I'm not much of a dancer, so I planned to wait until she took a break before speaking to her. After a while, she came over to the bar and ordered a drink for herself and her friend. Her eyes were bright blue, which were in stark contrast to her dark hair. Her skin was pale, and her lipstick, Russian red. Her features were even, and beautiful, a make-up artist's dream. The words on her T-shirt read: 'Smell of Female'.

As the barman was getting the drinks, I decided that if I was going to speak to her, now was as good a time as any. I knew she would be likely to think my approach was a chat up line, but I always carry some business cards, which have one of my photos printed on them. I avoided opening with, "Have you ever thought of becoming a model?" Instead, I introduced myself, and told her I was a photographer. I said that I always needed new models, and that she had a really good face that I wanted to photograph. She took the card and looked at the picture on it. She looked into my face, I think to make a judgement on my sincerity. She told me her name was Clara. I asked her to come to my studio sometime, to have a look around it. She said, "Let's go now, it'll be fun. Is it far?" I was surprised at her keen response, and desire to go to my studio at such a late hour. I asked her if she wanted to let her friend know where she was going, but she didn't seem too bothered about it.

She picked up her drink and took it with her into the cold, damp air. I told the taxi driver the address of my studio, and we were there in a few minutes. I always leave the heater on low so it was nice to get out of the cold.

I went to the plan chest and got my portfolio. We sat on the sofa, and she looked through my photographs, seemingly not paying much attention. She told me she liked them a lot, and that she definitely wanted to model for me. I suggested that I take a few polaroids of her, to see how she came out on film. I pulled down the colorama, and flooded it with light. As I loaded up my polaroid, Clara stepped into the light. Even before I was ready to shoot she began to move. She caressed her body lightly with her fingertips, following it's curves from her breasts to her thighs and back again, wiggling her hips. She asked me for some music and I turned on the tape. Then, she began to dance, rhythmically caressing her beautiful body, and moving to the music. She seemed totally unaware of me, or anything else.

I stood and watched, mesmerised. Her hair cascaded down to her shoulders, her hard nipples pierced the thin cotton of her T-shirt, and her fingers teased the zip on her hot pants up and down, letting me catch a glimpse of her white cotton panties. I put down the polaroid and picked up my 35mm, but shit, there was no film in it. So I had to be content with just watching. I'd shot two or three polaroids, and when the music stopped I showed them to her. She thought they were good, and asked if she could take one to show her girlfriend. She picked the one that was the most sexy and put it in her purse. We both got out our diaries and arranged the shoot for the following Friday at 6.00pm. Then she used her mobile phone to ring for a taxi, kissed me on the cheek, and left.

The next day I had some headshots to do, they are a bit boring but they pay the bills. Anyway, I showed the polaroids of Clara to Tricia, my make-up artist. Her eyes lit up.

"I must get my hands on that beautiful face," she said, "and what a body. You'd step over Elle Macpherson to get to that, wouldn't you Rick?"

She asked me when Clara was coming over, I told her it was all arranged for Friday. Friday was going to be busy as we had a girl-girl shoot for a magazine in the afternoon, and then Clara at 6.00pm.

Friday arrived. I spent the morning arranging the lights and setting the scene for the two-girl shoot. I had an old iron bedstead in front of a dark backdrop, thin cotton white sheets covered the mattress, and two big pillows were propped up at one end. I was going to use one overhead light, one main light and a fill-in to one side.

By two o'clock Tricia and the two models hadn't arrived. Tricia would take an hour to do their make-up, and the shoot would last a couple of hours, so time was getting a bit tight for finishing in time for Clara at six. I couldn't get her on her mobile to tell her to come later.

Tricia and the models, Sophie and Jane, finally arrived. They disappeared into the back room to begin the make-up, while I went to make us all coffee.

I had a final check round the studio set, and then looked through some books and magazines to get my creative juices flowing. I had laid out the clothes I wanted them to wear, so after the make-up was finished I told the girls what to put on. Sophie wore a short, sheer, tight lilac slip with white cotton panties underneath, and white hold up stockings. Jane put on a black lace push up bra, black French knickers, and black seamed stockings

I watched the two girls undress and dress. They were both blonde, with beautiful bodies, and being professional models, being naked in front of others was no big deal. I could see Tricia watching them with more than a professional eye. Sophie helped Jane with her suspenders and checked that the stocking seams were straight.

"Is this what you want Rick?" asked Jane.

"Yeah that's fine you look great," I replied, as I motioned to them to go over to the bed. "Sophie, kneel on the bed facing me. Jane, get behind Sophie and put your arms around her. Run your hands up and down her body and I'll take some shots. Both of you look into the camera."

The girls posed seductively on the bed and I began to shoot. The shutter opened and closed and the lights flashed as I pushed my finger on the button.

"Sophie, lick your top lip, and Jane open your mouth slightly. Good . . good. Sophie put your hands on Jane's breasts. Jane, you slide one hand down inside your knickers."

The girls obeyed. Both did exactly what I wanted, and no more. This was just a job to them. They had their well rehearsed model repertoire, which they had produced a hundred times before for other photographers. They were professional, they neither disliked nor enjoyed their job, they just did it. I was so looking forward to photographing Clara, who wouldn't need to be told every move to make, and who seemingly loved to perform.

"Sophie, move round and unfasten Jane's suspenders, and look up at Jane in a submissive way as you do it."

"Like this?" Sophie asked as she did what I told her.

"Yeah, good," I replied.

I finished the roll, and while I put in a new one, I asked Tricia to check the girls' hair and make-up. She climbed on to the bed with them and took a close look at each of their faces. I thought for a minute she was going to kiss Sophie, she got so close. Tricia touched up the lipstick with a brush, and then I was ready to shoot again.

I told Jane to take off her stockings before the next roll. Then I told both girls to kneel on the bed facing each other.

"Sophie, I want you to ease Jane's knickers down,

slowly. Peel them down gradually with your fingertips, and I'll get some shots of you doing that. Look into each others eyes longingly, and bring your faces in closer together, so that your lips nearly touch . . Jane take hold of Sophie's shoulder straps and pull down the slip so that you expose her breasts . . that's really good."

Tricia went downstairs to the kitchenette and came back with some ice. She gently caressed Sophie's nipples with the ice cubes to make them stand erect. Tricia really enjoys her job! When she finally got off the bed and out of view, I took up the camera and shot my second roll.

For the third roll, I told Sophie to remove her slip, leaving on her white knickers and hold ups. Jane still wore the black lace bra but nothing else.

"Jane, unclip your bra and let it fall away. Sophie, I need you to lick Jane's nipples for me," I said.

Tricia gave me a filthy look and put the ice bucket back on the table.

I got some great shots of Sophie sucking on Jane's nipples, and I asked Jane to pull down Sophie's knickers at the same time. Then I got them to kiss each other full on the lips, but as soon as they had begun kissing, my film roll ran out. I'd got so involved in the scene I'd lost track of how many shots I'd taken.

At that moment, Clara arrived. Tricia brought her up to the studio and explained that everything was running late. Tricia suggested Clara wait in the make-up room, but she was keen to sit and watch the rest of the shoot. She sat on a stool at the back of the studio. I apologised to

Clara for the delay and said it would only be about fifteen minutes. I asked Tricia to check Sophie and Jane's make-up once again and then began the final roll.

"Back to where we were girls. But, lose those stockings now Sophie, so that you are both totally naked."

Sophie obeyed, and the girls climbed back on the bed and knelt facing each other.

"Kiss each other passionately," I told them.

Their breasts rubbed together as they embraced and kissed. There was no need for Tricia's ice cubes as their nipples were hard and erect.

"Pull away slightly so that I can see your open mouths and tongues touching . . yeah great."

I glanced over at Clara. She looked even more stunning than she had the other night. She was leaning forward watching the girls intently. Tricia was sitting close to her. I asked Tricia to check the lipstick after the kissing, to make sure it hadn't smudged. After she had done this she immediately went back to sit with Clara.

"Sophie, I need you to lie back with your legs apart so that Jane can pretend to lick your pussy. And remember that the camera needs to see what is going on."

Again the girls obeyed and they looked great. Their bodies looked beautiful and their breasts were firm. As Sophie lay back I could tell that she had implants, as her breasts stood up. Whatever people say about implants, if they are done properly, and are not too large for the girl's physique, then they look really good.

In between shots, I looked over to Clara and Tricia.

They were both totally into it, staring at the sexy scene in front of them. Tricia was running her finger over her lips. I could tell she was getting really turned on. I'm sure that she would do her job for free if I didn't pay her.

"Jane, turn around now and slide backwards so that you're on top of Sophie . . . yeah that's right, so that you're in the 69 position."

I moved around the girls taking shots from different angles as the girls faked oral sex.

"Sophie, put your tongue as close to Jane's pussy as you can without touching it . . . good. Jane lift your head up and look at the camera. Give me an orgasmic expression . . . that's really good. Lick your lips. Open your mouth."

I shot the last pictures of the session with the girls faking orgasms. I told them they'd been really great, and that I was sure I had some excellent shots, enough for a magazine spread.

Sophie and Jane got dressed. They signed the model releases and I paid them. Clara came over and introduced herself to them.

"You two looked really cool when you were doing the shoot," she said. "Your boobs are fantastic Sophie, are they 100% natural or have you had a boob job?"

Sophie seemed taken aback by Clara's question, but answered, "Yeah, I used to be a 34B but now I'm a 34D. In this business you have to compete with so many other girls to get jobs, that you have to do whatever it takes. My boyfriend paid for them."

Clara was intent on finding out as much about these two models as she could, and seemed to be bursting with questions. And she didn't seem to worry about how personal they appeared to be. She turned to Jane and asked, "Did you really get as turned on as you looked when you were doing the photos just now? Will you two be doing it for real when you leave here?"

Jane looked surprised. "We just do what we're told to do," she replied tersely, giving the impression that it was none of Clara's business.

Clara was undaunted. "It turned me on watching you," she said. "I'm sure if I'd been doing that I would have to be doing it for real now."

I could see Tricia out of the corner of my eye. She had a wicked smile on her face, which totally gave away what she was fantasizing.

The models left, and Tricia began Clara's make-up. She loves to work on such a beautiful face, and spent over an hour relishing every minute. I heard a lot of giggling coming from the make-up room, so they must have been hitting it off. When Tricia had finished, Clara came out looking sensuous and sexy, and I couldn't wait to see her dressed in the outfits I had chosen. She came over to me, and as I was discussing the clothes with her, she began to undress. She discarded her skirt and top in a pile on the floor, and stood beside me in her bra and knickers. I told her to pick what she wanted to wear. She put on a short, half length, tight blue T-shirt, the roundness of her breasts showing where it finished, and a black lycra thong. At the other end of the studio I had set up a plain backdrop of white colorama. I told her to go and stand in front of it. Tricia put a tape on and immediately Clara began to move exactly as she had the other night. She moved her hips from side to side running her hands up and down her thighs, playing with her knickers, pulling them up so that they cut up into her pussy, her fingers disappearing occasionally under the black cotton, reaching further down every time.

I started to take pictures wanting to capture every delicious sexual moment on film. No words were spoken, they weren't needed. Clara's hand slid upwards over her tummy and over her breasts. She began to circle her nipples through her T-shirt with her fingertips, again just as they had done the other night they pierced the cotton. She started to pull the T-shirt up, revealing her beautiful firm ample bosom. I kept on shooting. She lifted the T-shirt up over her head and tossed it aside. Then running her fingers back down over her swollen nipples she thrust both hands down between her legs. Clara began to masturbate in front of us. She pulled the knickers aside and pushed her finger into herself, then out again, rubbing her clitoris in time to the music. She put her finger to her mouth and sucked it, tasting it's sweetness, before returning it to her pussy. She wriggled out of her knickers, easing them down to just above her knees. She turned around, arching her back and sticking her arse out for the camera. My film ran out, and as I turned to reload, I noticed Tricia leaning back against the studio wall. Her skirt was hitched up around her waist and her legs were slightly apart. Her hand was down the front of her panties and she was fingering herself. She was mesmerised by Clara, who still continued to masturbate, even though I wasn't shooting. Tricia suddenly stopped what she was doing when she realised I had seen her. She quickly pulled her skirt back down in to place.

Clara must have seen this, as she came straight over to Tricia, took her hand and led her to the bed. I switched on the lights again at that end of the studio, and quickly reloaded my camera. I could feel my erection straining against my jeans. But, like a true professional I carried on shooting!

Clara pushed Tricia gently backwards on to the bed. She began to remove Tricia's clothes. First, she unbuttoned her blouse and pulled it from her shoulders. Then she unclipped Tricia's bra and threw it to the floor. Then leaning forward, she took one nipple into her mouth and started to tease, flicking her tongue back and forth. Tricia sighed with pleasure. I thought to myself, Tricia must be in heaven, knowing how often she usually just swoons over the models, leaving herself frustrated. Clara pushed Tricia's skirt up to her waist and pulled off her pink satin panties, throwing them over towards me. It occurred to me that before I had been shooting the staged version with Sophie and Jane, but now I was viewing the real thing. The two women kissed deeply and passionately, Clara's hand slid between Tricia's legs and the fingers massaged her clitoris.

I was struggling with my desire to join them, but I wasn't sure if I'd be welcome. This was in conflict with an equal desire to keep watching. But, my tendency for voyeurism was winning the battle. No photographer worth his salt would waste an opportunity like this. This was not pretend, it was full-on sex.

Clara pushed two fingers into Tricia's mouth, letting her taste her own cunt juices. Then, kissed her again, tasting it herself. Tricia's hand went down between Clara's legs so they were both masturbating each other while they kissed. I don't think they even remembered that I was there, even though the lights kept flashing as the shutter of the camera opened and closed.

Clara slid down Tricia's body till her head was between Tricia's open thighs. Clara's tongue played gently with Tricia's clit. It wasn't long before Tricia was ready to come. She screamed with pleasure and pushed Clara's head down harder into her pussy, curling her fingers around Clara's hair. Tricia gripped the sheets at each side of her pulling them taught as she came, letting out small gasps of delight. I'd captured everything on film. Tricia lay back on the bed and closed her eyes to relax.

Clara turned to me and asked me to get her bag from the chair. I did as she asked and brought it to her. She opened it and took out a small square condom packet. She looked up at me and smiled suggestively.

"Do you want to?" she asked.

I unbuttoned my jeans as an answer to her question, and kicked them aside. She tore open the packet and pulled out the rubber condom. She placed it carefully on the tip of my erect penis and rolled it down the shaft. I lay on the bed and she climbed on top of me. She straddled me and guided my cock into her tight pussy. I was glad of the condom as without it I would have come straight away. She wriggled and undulated on top of me squealing with delight. I reached out to touch her heaving breasts as they swayed in front of me. They were real, and they were fantastic. I held them as she rode up and down on me, my cock sliding in and out of her. Then she got off me and knelt with her hands on the iron bedstead, sticking out her arse for me to take her from behind. I noticed Tricia had the polaroid and was busy taking shots of us from various angles. I was too turned on to care. I reached forward to stimulate Clara's clitoris while I entered her pussy from behind. She responded by pushing herself backwards and forwards on to my cock. I could feel my orgasm building inside me, and Clara's panting was getting faster and faster.

"I can't go on Rick . . I'm going to come . . ." she gasped.

"Yeah, now, now . . ." I said.

"Rub my clit . . harder, harder . . ."

Clara pushed herself back towards me, pushing my cock deeper and deeper into her as she came. My cum gushed into the condom.

We both fell back on to the bed, exhausted. Tricia snapped a last polaroid and exclaimed, "That's a wrap. I think I got what I needed." We all burst out laughing.

Bettina writes,

At the garage where I get my car serviced, there's a mechanic called Dave who always chats me up when I take my car in.

One day I left some of my manuscripts on the back seat, and I wondered if he had read them when he serviced my car.

The next time I took my car in, I found this story, in a plain brown envelope in my glove compartment. A small note was attached, saying it was from a girl called Olivia. But going by the oily fingerprints on the envelope, I think it may have been from Dave. I mentioned it to him and offered to pay him for the story. He just winked at me and smiled.

Cheap & Dirty

CHEAP & DIRTY

Olivia picked up her keys along with her mobile phone and her black velvet bag. The small bag bulged with her make up, all her credit and store cards, and her rubber filofax (it wasn't politically correct to have a leather one these days). She swept past the coat stand collecting her jacket, and opened the front door of her studio flat.

Downstairs in the basement she walked towards her car, admiring it as she got nearer. She knew that it had got her noticed in the six months since she bought it, and it gave her a real buzz driving it around. When she first saw it in her local garage, she knew she had to have it. She'd always wanted a sports car and this one was a delicious red colour. It had an open top and wire wheels, and it was a bargain that Olivia wasn't prepared to miss. So far she hadn't been disappointed, it drove like a dream. And, although it drank juice and meant higher insurance, she adored it. As it was a classic she wanted to look after it, so she had booked it in for a full service.

When she arrived at the garage, she checked the car in, and was told to drive it around the back to the mechanic. She parked the car outside the working area, walked back to the waiting room and picked up a magazine.

Half an hour passed and Olivia began to get impatient. She lit a cigarette and had a coffee that looked like mud out of the machine.

After nearly an hour, she thought she would try to find someone to ask how much longer she would have to wait. There was no one around, and the receptionist had disappeared. She decided to walk round to the mechanic to see how he was getting on, or if he'd even started on her car.

Slipping in between cars she peered into the darkness of the garage, and seeing her car up on the ramp, she walked towards it, her stiletto heels clicking on the oily concrete. She leaned forward slightly to see if the mechanic was under her car, but finding no one there, she ventured further into the dimly lit building. Feeling rather silly she began to call out, "Hello," in a manner that suggested she felt that she was trespassing. But just as she was about to leave, she turned to find the mechanic standing directly behind her. She gasped, more from surprise than fear, and looked him up and down. He was tall and in his mid twenties. His hair was jet black and cropped tight to his head, and he was unshaven. He was oily and unkempt, and looked more than a little rough. She noticed the tatoos on his muscular forearms. A busty naked woman was displayed on his right arm, and on his left he had a blue lion with 'Chelsea FC' written underneath. She was amazed to find that she rather liked them, despite having always thought that tatoos were rather common and vulgar. She found herself attracted to this swarthy man standing in front of her. Although she usually preferred a cleaner more washed sort of guy, there was something very sexual about him that she found quite irresistible. Even his oily, dirty smell seemed good, and she blushed as her eyes worked their way up his body, finally meeting his.

"Do you have tattoos all over your body?" Olivia asked, desperate for something to say that might account for her having stared at him for so long.

"On my back," he replied gruffly, "wanna see?"

Olivia hesitated for a second before nodding her head. He immediately began removing his oily overalls, revealing a bare and muscled chest which was so much cleaner than his clothes. He turned his back towards her, and she saw that he had a beautiful mermaid painted across his shoulders. Turning back he said, "Are your tits as good as hers?"

Olivia blushed some more.

"Can I see?" he asked, thrusting an oily hand towards her. Olivia took a step back. He was so dirty and her clothes were so clean and crisp. If he touched her white blouse it would be ruined. He stepped close to her and his fingers reached out for the top button on her blouse. He undid the first button. Olivia felt a warmth flood through her body. Her pussy began to feel hot. She wanted him to touch her, but was at the same time repulsed by the thought of such oily hands on her clean skin. He undid all the buttons and opened the front of her blouse revealing her breasts. They were big and rounded and were pushed into her tight fitting bra.

"Wow! Nice," he exclaimed. His large dirty hands cupped her breasts and squeezed them. Olivia's body tingled and her nipples began to harden. His fingers pinched them through the silky bra and they hardened even more under his confident touch. How brash just to touch me in this way, Olivia thought. But she didn't want him to stop. His fingers moved to the front clip of the bra, and deftly unclipped it. He pulled the bra open to expose Olivia's beautiful pert breasts for his inspection.

"Fucking nice tits," he said, staring at them admiringly. "I'd like to get my prick between them. In fact that's not the only place I'd like to get my prick right now."

Olivia felt her pussy begin to throb. He was staring into her eyes and she blushed again. She felt sure he could tell how turned on she was. Pulling her blouse together, she said, "Well, really! I don't know what kind of girl you think I am, but . . ."

Before she could finish her sentence his open mouth was over hers. His rough kisses aroused her even more, as his stubbled chin rubbed against her face and his tongue searched deep inside her mouth. His hands pushed her breasts together.

"You need a good fuck don't you - that's what you've come for," he said. He leaned down and with his hand he guided Olivia's erect nipple into his mouth. He began sucking it and gently biting it. His other hand moved down her body towards the hem of her skirt. Olivia's pussy was so wet and hot. More than anything she wanted his hand to travel up, under her skirt to find it. His strong hand ran up to the top of her thigh and then slid between her legs.

"You're so fucking wet, you horny little bitch, you must really want it bad." He slipped his fingers inside her panties and rubbed her clitoris. Olivia writhed at his touch.

He unzipped his jeans and his large erection pushed it's way through the open fly. Pushing Olivia downwards to kneel in front of him he pressed the tip of his hard cock against her mouth.

"Come on babe, suck it," he said.

Olivia opened her mouth and he pushed his cock inside.

"Suck me baby, suck me," he demanded. Olivia began to suck on the huge erection. It was so big. It went deep inside her mouth and she sucked hard on it. He thrust it into her and began to get faster, till she thought he was going to come in her mouth. But then he withdrew and said, "Now turn around, I want to fuck your tight little cunt." Olivia turned around and knelt facing away from him, her pussy soaking wet with the anticipation of him entering her. He knelt behind her and used his muscled thigh to open her legs wide apart. He pushed only the tip of his cock into her waiting pussy and then he stopped. Olivia pushed back to get his penis inside her, but he pulled it away again, just letting the tip tease her entrance.

"What do you want me to do now?" he asked. "Do you want me to fuck you? You do don't you? You're gagging for it aren't you? . . . . *Aren't you?*"

"Yes," said Olivia with a desperate tone in her voice.

"Well tell me what you want and I'll give it to you."

"I want you to fuck me . . . please," whispered Olivia.

"I can't hear you," he said, pushing his cock into Olivia's cunt for a few hard thrusts and then stopping again.

"I want you to fuck me . . . *fuck me now!* . . please . . I need it *now,* " begged Olivia.

"Okay then if that's what you want you fucking bitch whore."

He thrust his cock into Olivia's hot cunt, roughly pulling her hips towards him. The feelings of ecstasy filled her body as his hard shaft penetrated her deeply.

"Do you like it baby? You fucking slut, you love it hard, right up your cunt, don't you, you fucking slag. Tell me how much you love it bitch."

"I love it. Please don't stop. I've never had it like this, you make me so hot," she answered.

Then with one final thrust, she felt his cock explode it's hot cum into her. With one cruel tug he withdrew, leaving her kneeling, frustrated, on all fours. Pushing her aside he said, "Your car's ready. I'll get Jeff to drive it round the front for you. You can pay at reception."

Bettina writes,

When I was last in New York, I was in a bar, and I heard a policeman telling some of his drinking buddies about an alleged crime that he had been called to.

I'll let you read it, before telling you what the cop thought really happened . . .

Power Dressing

POWER DRESSING

She opened her wardrobe and took her long leather coat from the hanger, laying it carefully on her bed. Then undressing, she admired her reflection in the mirror on the bedroom wall. She chose her underwear with care from the large selection in the chest of drawers beside the bed. She picked out a tight fitting basque in red taffeta with black lace, suspenders, and a new pair of sheer black seamed stockings to go with her new shiny black stilettos.

She sat at her vanity mirror and began to apply her make-up. Paying attention to her eyes first and then her lips. She pouted at her herself, smiled and dressed, stroking the silky black material of her stockings, as she rolled them gently up to the fasteners on her firm thighs, and pulling the basque to lace it up as tightly as she could bear, accentuating her breasts and tiny waist.

She brushed her hair until it shone, then swept it all up into a pleat, leaving soft tendrils framing her face. Then she took the coat from the bed and put it on, tying the belt round her waist, and checking her reflection in the mirror to make sure that no one could see underneath it. Then, satisfied that she looked as good as she could, she left the house and began to walk into town.

She felt confident and poised as she got near to her target, and when she turned the corner and saw the shop in front of her, she felt a flutter of exhilaration. It was too late to turn back now, she must go through with it. From the pavement she checked to make sure that there were no customers in the shop.

Silently, she opened the shop door and stepped inside, changing the sign from 'open' to 'closed'. A man's voice called out from the back, "May I help you?" She walked towards it smiling. A man appeared in the doorway. From her pocket she pulled out a gun and pointed it at him, ordering him to turn around. She pushed him back through the doorway, and told him to lie down.

"There's money in the till if you want it, take it. Just don't hurt me. I've got a wife and two kids," he said.

Untying her belt, she slid it from it's loops as her coat fell to the floor.

"I don't want your money. I want you," she said. "Take off your clothes."

He undid his tie and took it off, followed by his shirt and then his trousers. Stopping at his boxer shorts he asked, "What's your problem lady?"

"And the rest," she ordered.

He removed his boxer shorts, and he stood naked and vulnerable in front of her.

"Lie down on your back with your hands round the table leg," she demanded.

"What are you going to do to me?"

"Shut up and do as I say, and you won't get hurt."

Before he had time to say anything more, she gagged him with a scarf that she had pulled from her cleavage. She tied his hands above his head with the belt from her coat and secured them to the table leg. She reached for a piece of rope from one of the pockets of her coat, and with it she tied his feet together. Satisfied that there was no way he could escape, she opened her legs and stood over his face, revealing her soaking wet pussy. She plunged her fingers into it's damp warmth, and began to play with herself, occasionally licking her sweet juices from her fingers. She looked down at his naked body.

"Now I'm going to make your prick rock hard, and you're not going to be able to do a thing about it," she said.

She knelt down beside him, took his cock in her hand, and began to massage it up and down between her fingers. It began to harden despite his muffled protests. Then slowly she began to caress him, letting her tongue flick gently all over his body, biting at his cherry red nipples, and then down to his pubic hair, and further, till it reached the tip of his penis. She opened her mouth and gently she licked the end of his cock as she looked up at his face. She teased, not taking too much inside her mouth. Her tongue circled, gently pressing against the sensitive tip. Her hands stroked his muscular chest and her fingernails scratched at his flesh. He moaned, and strained to push himself further inside her mouth, but she pulled away. She leisurely undid the laces on her basque, watching to see the look on his face. She undid the last hook, freeing her large rounded breasts which she pressed against his chest. She knelt astride his engorged cock and rode him till waves of passion engulfed her body and she came. She was surprised that he hadn't orgasmed at the same time as her, so she climbed off him and began to suck at his huge erection, lingering over the sweet tastes of her own juices. She let him thrust himself deep into her throat and she could feel waves of passion building in his penis. She licked at it harder and harder, letting her tongue slip all the way down it's throbbing shaft. Finally, she felt his hot cum shoot into her throat and she drank it down greedily. After his spasms of pleasure died down, she lay next to him and played with her pussy, pushing her fingers deep inside and then rubbing her clitoris. Once more she felt her orgasm flood through her body and now she was satisfied. After a minute or two, she got to her feet, and taking some tissues from a box on the desk, she cleaned herself up and began to dress.

When she was ready, she put on her leather coat, and smoothing it down she tied it tightly once more. She bent over and kissed him gently on the forehead. She returned to the shop front, and checking that the street was empty, she turned the sign back to 'open', and left unobserved as quickly and as quietly as she had arrived. It amused her to think about him being found in the back room, stark naked, and tied to his desk just like the last one. What would the papers make of this second attack? The word 'attack' hardly seemed appropriate, this one hadn't struggled at all, but now she had to move on and find another quiet shop, with just one male assistant and a comfy back room. She laughed to herself as she walked off in the direction of home.

Bettina writes,

The cop was sure that the naked guy he found wasn't telling the whole truth. Being seduced at gunpoint by a beautiful woman was a little to much for him to believe.

He suspected that the real story was more like - the guy gets horny and calls for a hooker, she ties him up for a little kinky sex play, but instead of having sex, she robs him.

Bettina writes,

Last summer I attended a Writers Seminar at a University. They had asked me to give a lecture on my personal interest in Erotica. After the lecture a guy called Mark came to me and we talked for ages. He was really cute. I shouldn't say it as I know he will read this but I really had the hots for him! Anyway, I asked him about his sexual experiences. He had something interesting going on, and the following story is how it began . . .

French Lessons

FRENCH LESSONS

Mark heard the post drop through the letterbox and hit the mat. He picked up the pile of letters and leaflets and rifled through it, hoping not to find that expected brown envelope. He knew he was going to have to find out some time, but it made his stomach churn to think of it. There, amongst the junk mail and the news from home for the other students, was the small manila holder of his fate. Mark stared at it. If he'd failed this exam his parents were going to be so pissed at him. They'd paid for everything, his accommodation, his food, his spending money and all his course fees. They had so much invested in his doing well, and pushed him all the time to apply himself. But, he knew he hadn't worked hard enough. He spent far more time in the pub with his mates than in the library. And the thought of a weekend in Brighton with his friends at college down there had always been much more inviting than the prospect of working on his assignments. He'd promised his parents faithfully that he was studying hard, and he'd lied about his essay marks. If he passed this exam it would be miracle. Unable to face discovering the worst, Mark slipped the envelope into his back pocket. Finding out later would be soon enough.

At college he listened to students congratulating each

other. He kept a low profile so nobody would get the chance to ask him how he did.

When everyone had gone to lectures and the canteen was nearly empty he decided to find out one way or the other. He took the envelope out of his pocket and slipped his fingers under the flap. As he pulled the little slip of paper from the envelope, the word 'Fail' came into view.

"Shit!" he said, flicking the paper across the floor. "What the hell am I going to do now?" The thought of resitting in a months time was so depressing, especially when he expected to do little better than before.

Mark looked across to the coffee machine wondering if he had enough change. One of the canteen girls, Tracy, was wiping the machine with a cloth, but seemed to be paying more attention to Mark than to what she was doing.

"Didn't do as well as you'd hoped?" she said sympathetically.

"No. I fucking failed," said Mark, not in the mood to be polite.

"Are you going to resit then?" she persisted.

"What's the fucking point? I'll only fail again," said Mark.

"Well, maybe you could get some extra tuition. On the pin board there's a card of a private tutor. I've heard that she's really good. She helps you cover the main things and gets you through the exam. It's worth a try."

"There's no point, I've only got a month before the resit. There's no way I'll be ready by then."

Mark delved into his pocket searching for change, but he didn't have the right coins for the coffee machine.

"Fucking hell Tracy, look I haven't even got the right money to buy a coffee. I'm totally useless!"

Tracy looked across to Mark, "Come into the kitchen and I'll make you a coffee. It'll be nicer than a machine one. Come on, there's nobody in there, so I won't get into trouble."

Mark walked across to Tracy and she led the way behind the canteen counter into the kitchen. It was a really big kitchen where all the cooking was done for the students meals. Everything seemed to be made of stainless steel and every surface was totally clean. Tracy picked up the electric kettle and went to the sink to fill it with water. She turned on the tap a little too fast, and water splashed everywhere, drenching the front of her T-shirt. She stepped back. "Oh shit, look what I've done," she said, turning towards Mark. She had no bra under her top, so it clung to her breasts, making them clearly visible through the wet cotton. Her nipples stood out, erect from the coldness of the water.

"You could enter next week's wet T-shirt competition!" he said, laughing. "I'd give you ten out of ten."

"Oh yeah, I'm sure I would have a chance," Tracy replied sarcastically. "I'm not eighteen anymore, I'm twenty-nine. I'll be thirty next month. Compared to those girl students you hang around with, I'm sure you think I'm past it!"

"No, you're in great shape," said Mark coming across

to where Tracy stood. "You've got a gorgeous figure." Mark reached out his hands towards Tracy's wet breasts, wondering for a moment if she would push him away. She didn't, and his hands cupped her firm round bosoms. He felt the hard nipples nestle in the palms of his hands, and he squeezed gently, leaning forward to kiss her mouth.

"Wait," said Tracy, pulling away from his lips. Mark let go of her, thinking he had been rejected. Tracy went to the door and turned the key to lock it. Walking back towards Mark, she smiled and said, "Now we won't be interrupted." She reached up to release her blonde hair, which was pinned up tidily on top of her head. It fell down loosely around her shoulders and she ran her fingers through it. She pulled the bottom of her T-shirt up freeing it from the tight skirt band into which it was tucked. As she took it off over her head, Mark leaned forward and took one of her nipples in his mouth, sucking and teasing it with his tongue. His hands were feeling Tracy's arse, massaging it through her skirt. He lifted the skirt up and slid his hands inside her knickers so that he could feel her soft smooth buttocks. Tracy pulled his head away from her breasts and they kissed passionately once more. Tracy's fingers tried desperately to undo the buttons on Mark's shirt, but before she had finished, he lifted her up on to the edge of the table, pushing her skirt up and pulling off her knickers. He undid his belt buckle and unzipped his fly, pushing his trousers and pants down below his hips, releasing his rampant cock. Tracy feverishly grabbed his erection and pulled it towards her waiting pussy. She wrapped her legs around his waist and lay back on the table as he pushed his cock deep inside her tight cunt. She gasped for breath with every thrust, and grabbed the sides of the table to stop herself from sliding backwards, as she wanted to feel his whole length inside her. Mark slid his hand down to find her clitoris. As he touched it and began lightly to rub it, Tracy pushed her body towards his touch. He rubbed faster and harder and she began to come. He watched her orgasm and she pushed her pussy faster up and down his shaft, and pressed her clitoris harder against his fingers. His cock pulsed and filled with semen. He grabbed her thighs and pulled her tight up against him as he pumped his cum inside her.

Quickly they dressed. Tracy unlocked the door but seemed reluctant to return to her boring duties after such a distraction. "Mark, that was fantastic. You wouldn't fail an exam in fucking!"

Mark's mind spun back to the exam problem. But it didn't weigh so heavily on him as it had done earlier. Shooting his load had lightened his mood. He decided to check out the bulletin board, and crossed the canteen to the foyer. He searched amongst the adverts until he found the card Tracy had talked about. It read:

PERSONAL TUITION
from
Experienced Private Tutor.
All the instruction you need.
Call Madeline for more information.

Mark thought that Madeline sounded like a nice friendly kind of name, so he scribbled the phone number on the back of his hand. He went to his room to get a phone card so he could call her before he had a chance to change his mind.

He dialled the number apprehensively.

"Madeline speaking, how can I help?" came the voice. It was soft and soothing, and Mark already began to feel better.

"My name is Mark. I've just failed my exam and I really need some help to get through the resit. I saw your card on the notice board and I wondered if . . ."

"Yes darling, of course," reassured Madeline. "You must come and see me and I will help you any way I can. Come tomorrow at around seven. Okay?"

"Yes, okay," said Mark, "see you then."

Replacing the receiver, Mark felt relieved that he had actually done something positive for once. Madeline sounded so nice. He went off to his afternoon lecture wondering what she would be like.

The next evening he cycled to the address Madeline had given him. He padlocked his bike to the railings and knocked on the door. He nearly dropped all his books when the door opened and a stunning woman stood in the doorway.

"I've come to see Madeline," he said, not at all sure that this was her.

"That's me sweetheart," she said kindly. "Come in won't you?"

She was tall and beautiful. Mark guessed she was around thirty five. Her hair was long and red, and tied back in a pony tail that left soft wisps of curls falling gently across her face. Her complexion was pale ivory and her eyes were green. Mark stood outside still rooted to the spot.

"Come on then, I don't bite you know. Well, not unless you really want me to . ." said Madeline smiling. She took Mark's hand and led him inside. They entered a large and comfortable room with lots of throws and cushions scattered around. Mark felt rather embarrassed about his drippy behaviour thus far. He tried to assert himself a little, "Thanks for seeing me", he said sitting on the sofa, "I've brought my books in case we can start tonight."

Madeline sat down close beside him. Her warm sexy body pressed against his. Her hair was close to his face and he breathed in it's fresh and sensuous aroma. Her dress was low cut, showing lots of pale rounded cleavage, and it's hem was short revealing long smooth bare legs. Mark began to feel distinctly aroused by her and wasn't looking forward to being in close proximity to such a beautiful woman that he couldn't have. The frustration was going to be unbearable, let alone the problem of disguising his erection that he knew he would have before long. He opened a large book in his lap, and tried to think about the work that he so desperately needed to concentrate on.

Madeline began to talk about course work, and leaned forward to reach for a pen on the table. Mark felt his cock stir as he looked at her breasts. He told himself to think of something else, but then he began to imagine her nakedness beneath her clothes. His cock grew hard under his fly. 'Think of the work, the work,' he said in his head.

"Which bit are you having the most problems with?" Madeline asked. "What would you like me to help you with most?"

Mark's mind raced: 'My cock,' he thought, 'that's what I want you to help me with; that's the bit I'm having the trouble with. If you could just suck it for me, and then if you could just put your pussy on to it for me and ride me like a . . .' His thoughts were interrupted by the telephone ringing. Madeline got up to answer it and left the room.

Mark tried to collect himself while she was gone. He knew he'd never learn anything at this rate. Why did she have to be so beautiful? Tutors aren't usually sexy, he thought to himself, they're usually like old aunties you haven't seen for years. He counted backwards from fifty, and then tried to remember all the players in the Southampton football team - anything to take his mind off sex. His erection finally disappeared and Madeline returned to sit beside him again.

"Sorry about that interruption," she said. "Now let's see where were we . ."

They spent about an hour going over some course work, and then Madeline said she could lend Mark some books to take home with him. She walked across to the bookshelf and looked through some of the spines. She put her finger to her lips as she thought about which books to choose. Then she started to look at the lower shelves. As she bent down to run her fingers along the books, Mark could see that she had no panties on. He caught a glimpse of her buttocks, and then as she turned, he saw just a hint of her pussy. His cock stood to attention and he put his hands across his lap to cover it. How could she do this to him, he thought, teaching him one minute, and then bending down with no panties on the next. He decided it was time to leave. He got up and started to gather his stuff. "I think it's about time I got off," he said.

Madeline looked surprised and a little disappointed. "Won't you stay a bit longer," she purred, walking across to him. "You've been looking at me all evening." There was warmth and a little amusement in her tone. "I think maybe you want to fuck me?"

Mark blushed.

"Well, you do, don't you baby?" she asked, sliding her hand down his body towards his fly. When her fingers reached the bulge in his jeans they pressed downwards, travelling the length of his erection and back towards his belt again. "Ooh, baby, you do want to fuck me," she whispered, pushing her breasts against Mark's chest and drawing her lips close to his as she spoke. "You're so hard. You must want to get your prick inside me real bad. I bet you've been imagining my pussy haven't you, and how you'd like it tight around your prick."

Madeline undid the buttons on Mark's shirt and slipped it off his shoulders and down his arms, letting it drop to the floor. She ran her hands over his bare chest and leaned forward to kiss him gently on the lips. "Turn around," she said. Mark did as she asked. He felt her tying his wrists together with something like a scarf or a stocking. The feeling of being restrained by her excited him even more than ever and his erection pulsed inside his fly.

"Face me", she ordered. Mark did as he was told. She pushed him and he fell backwards into the leather armchair. Madeline stood before him. "This is what you want isn't it baby?" She slowly pulled her dress up revealing her pussy for Mark to see. "Isn't it beautiful?" she asked.

"Yes it's beautiful," said Mark admiring the small triangle of soft fine pubic hair.

"I'm going to let you watch while I touch myself. Do you like to watch baby?"

"Yes", Mark replied. He couldn't believe this was happening. It was one of those situations you only read about in trashy paperbacks. And when you're reading you think it's all pure fiction.

Madeline sat in the chair opposite and spread her legs. "See how wet I am Mark?" Madeline used two fingers to spread her pussy lips apart revealing her inner redness. Then she pushed both fingers deep inside. "Oh that feels so good . . imagine your cock inside me Mark . . imagine yourself shafting me, pumping hard into me with your gorgeous prick. Oh yes baby! Harder, harder!" Madeline threw her head back, with both hands she rubbed her clit.

After a few minutes, Madeline stopped what she was doing, opened her eyes and said, "Oh you poor baby, sitting way over there. What must you think of me? What kind of host am I? Your cock must be so hard, and all cramped up in those tight jeans. Stand up and come over here you poor boy, and I'll help you out of them."

Mark struggled to his feet and walked over to where Madeline sat. She began to unbuckle his belt. He didn't know what she was going to do to him and his heart pounded with anticipation.

"You'll feel a lot better when I free your cock". Madeline unzipped his fly and pulled his jeans and underpants down over his hips. Mark looked down at his erection. It was stiff and upright and it was only a couple of inches away from her mouth. He had never had a women take him inside her mouth before. He begged her in his mind to put it in her mouth and suck it. She took his penis in her hand and began to rub it playfully, admiring it's form and thickness. "You have such a lovely cock," she said. "It's so hard, and so ready for me to suck it. Do you want me to suck it baby? I will if you want me to. Do you want me to?"

"Yes," he said urgently.

"Yes what?"

"Yes please," he replied with a begging tone, "please suck it for me."

"That's better baby, good manners never hurt anyone. Of course I will suck it for you since you asked me so nicely." Madeline licked the length of Mark's penis, holding the base between her finger and thumb. Mark sighed, the touch of her tongue felt amazing to him. She teased his penis with little licks, and she curled her tongue around it's tip. Her lips parted to take in the end of his cock, and then she gradually let it slip right in. It went in and out of her mouth. Mark looked down. He could see her head moving backwards then forwards, his cock in this beautiful woman's mouth. It felt fantastic, even better he thought than a pussy. She sucked him harder. He wanted to come, to come in her mouth. It was something he'd always fantasized about. Now she had his whole length, sucking and playing with it with her tongue. Mark could feel his spunk start to rise at the base of his cock. There was no way he could hold back any longer. His cum shot out into Madeline's throat, with every thrust more white spunk spurted into her mouth. Expertly she drank every drop until he was totally spent. She released his penis. Some of his semen had oozed from her mouth on to her lips, she wiped her mouth with the back of her hand.

"Now Mark, drop to your knees. I want you to kneel in front of me." Mark did as she asked. Madeline parted her thighs to expose her cunt. Her fingers began to rub her clitoris. "I want you to lick and suck at my clit, will you do that for me baby?"

"Yes," he replied.

Madeline lifted her pussy up towards his face. Mark leaned forward, his hands still tied tightly behind his back. His tongue found the mound of her clit, and he started to tease it with his tongue, flicking it back and forth, biting the soft flesh tenderly. Madeline's breathing became heavy. "Ooh that's it baby," she gasped. Mark's tongue explored her sex, tasting the sweet juices. With her fingers she spread her pussy lips. "Lick me out," she demanded. He did as he was told, licking and sucking at the glistening wetness oozing from her pussy. It was so erotic being told what to do to her, and the feel of her pussy in his mouth was arousing his penis once more.

"Now I must have your prick inside me. Is it ready to give me what I need?" she said, looking down to see his cock standing stiffly away from his body. "Oh it's ready and waiting." She reached down and grasped his penis tightly in her hand, "It's so hard! I must have it," she said. "Sit on the chair over there."

Mark got up and went to sit on a small low chair that she had pointed to. Madeline came to him and sat astride his lap. Sliding her legs around his waist, she lowered herself on to his cock.

"Ooh that feels lovely," she said, guiding his erection into her pussy with her hand. Her fingers played with her clitoris as she rode him, faster and faster. "I'm coming," she cried, pushing herself harder on to his penis. She kissed him and bit into his lip. "Oh yeah, fuck me harder. I want your cock to spurt into my cunt." Mark climaxed almost immediately, his hot spunk shooting upwards inside her.

Madeline freed Mark's wrists. He rubbed them where the scarf had dug into him. He picked up his clothes and began to dress. Madeline slipped on a silky gown that she took from a drawer.

"Well darling," she said, "Let me see how you've done this evening." Madeline reclined on the sofa and thought for a few moments with her finger to her lips. "Your French is very good," she said, smiling. "You are a quick learner. However, you will need to be trained. You'll need many more sessions if I am to turn you into a well disciplined student. Your education is just beginning, and I will be your mistress."

Bettina writes,

I have to raise issue with the title of the next story. I'm not bad, I'm very, very good!

All women are bad

ALL WOMEN ARE BAD

George left the conference room to find a phone. He'd arranged to call his wife at six o'clock, and now it was nearly eight. These things always went on much longer than expected. He hated leaving his wife to go on business trips even for a couple of days. This was his fourth trip since Christmas and he felt sure that she was feeling neglected, and maybe even seeing someone else.

The phones in the hotel lobby were being used, so he strolled out into Regent Street to find a nearby call box. He found two phone boxes side by side, both were occupied. While he waited outside for one to become free he looked at the back wall of the phone booth. It was covered in coloured postcards advertising every different kind of prostitute available. There was something for everyone, no matter what their fantasy or fetish. From dominatrix to school girls, from 'genuine' virgins to horny biker chicks. Some needed a 'firm hand' while others offered to 'discipline naughty boys'. Most of the cards had photographs on them, some even claimed to be 'genuine' photos of the girls. George read them all, and to pass the time he considered which girl he would choose to have sex with. He wasn't into spanking or being spanked, and golden showers left him cold. Although he liked big

breasts, he didn't want the services of the milk maid. He also didn't fancy the dominatrix; whips and chains and handcuffs, and rubber from head to toe. He liked the look of the biker chick, hot pants and knee high leather boots, but maybe she was still a little too threatening. Then he saw her - the girl of his dreams. His choice was made, and there was no doubt in his mind. She was absolutely beautiful, with thick, shoulder length dark hair and big blue eyes. Her skin was smooth, soft and tanned. She looked like she was approachable too, not hard like some of the girls in the other pictures. Her body was built for sex. She had ample breasts that you would die for. They looked firm and enticing. Just begging for his cock to squeeze between them, he thought. He started fantasizing how they would feel around his penis, soft and warm and tight. And how his cum would splash all over them. How she would love it!

One of the booths became free and George's thoughts returned to his wife. As he lifted the receiver he wondered for a moment what he would do if she was having an affair. What if she'd got a lover with her right now? He told himself not to be so silly, that he was probably being paranoid. But doubts kept going through his mind. Recently her behaviour had changed, and isn't that the first sign that your partner is having an affair? She didn't seem to miss him as much as she used to, and their sex life had waned. She seemed to be taking more care of her appearance, wearing more make-up, and fussing over her hair. On his return from his last trip away, he noticed new sexy lingerie in her underwear drawer. When he had mentioned it she just said she had treated herself. He couldn't help suspecting that another man had bought it for her.

He reached into his pocket for some change and dialled the number. It rang for some time, and he was just about to put the receiver down thinking that she had gone out when it was answered.

"Hello."

"Hello Kim, sorry I'm late calling. How are you darling?" asked George.

"I'm fine, keeping myself busy, you know how it is. How's the conference going?" said Kim, a little disjointedly.

George hesitated for a moment. "You sound out of breath, are you okay?" he asked.

"Oh, I was changing the sheets on the bed when the phone rang, so I had to run to the phone. How's the conference, are you having a good time and making lots of new contacts?"

"Oh, it's not bad. I'd rather be home with you. It's been rather boring today. I met a guy called Richard, who might give me some business, but nothing concrete, you know how people talk."

"I'd better go, I've got some pasta cooking . . ." Kim sounded flustered, and eager to get off the phone.

George heard a voice in the background. It sounded like the words, "Come on angel, I haven't got long."

"Who was that?"

"Oh, that's just the TV. I'm watching a soap. Well, I

must go now. When will you be coming home?"

"I'll be back on Saturday, about tea time. See you then. Bye love."

"See you. Bye."

Kim put down the phone. George stood there with the receiver still in his hand. How could his wife be making the bed, cooking pasta and watching television, all at the same time? She sounded so distracted and keen to get off the phone. The telephone was a long way from the television, and he was sure in his own mind that the voice he had heard was her secret lover. He decided to call her straight back and have it out with her, he just couldn't go through the night wondering what she was getting up to in his bed.

He dialled the number again. This time it just rang and rang. "The bitch," he said, slamming down the phone. "She's fucking around on me." George leaned back against the door of the phone box. He began to imagine his wife on all fours, a man behind her, fucking her while she begged for more. Then she turned around and knelt in front of him, sucking on his dick till he shot his cum over her face and in her mouth. "Fucking slut!" shouted George.

He stared at the back wall of the phone booth. The cards gradually came into focus, and his eyes fell on his dream girl. George grabbed the card. "It's my turn to have some fun," he said. George knew he had to make the call now before he changed his mind, and he felt in his pocket for some more coins. Pulling some out he pushed them hurriedly into the slot and dialled the number on the card.

After a few rings, it was answered by a woman.

"Hello, can I help you?"

"I saw your advert in Regent Street, and I wondered if I could arrange a hotel visit? Could you give me some details?"

"Yes. We have four girls today. Blanche who is a twenty-three year old blonde, lovely figure, 34B-24-36, loves being submissive. Tina is a redhead, very voluptuous, twenty years old, very tall, 36C-24-36. She caters for most tastes. Raquel is a new girl, only been here a couple of weeks. She is new to this kind of work, but she's very enthusiastic, and very open minded. Our last girl is Andrea. She is from the Mediterranean and she has lovely dark skin. Her measurements are 38DD-26-36. Lovely long legs and tall too, she's five foot ten. Her speciality is body to body massage. Would you like to go ahead and book one of the girls sir?"

"Well, they all sound very nice, but I was rather hoping to book Janey. Is she available?"

"Well, it's her night off. Are you sure you don't want to try one of the other girls? They are all lovely."

"No. I think I'll leave it. Thanks anyway."

"Wait . . I may be able to reach her on her mobile and see if she is free. It may cost a bit more though . . ."

"I don't mind paying extra, I really want her."

"Okay then sir, give me a moment. If you hold the line I will try to get hold of her."

George waited. His heart was racing. He hadn't felt like this in a long while. It felt dangerous and that excited him. The woman came back on to the line.

"You are in luck sir, I have talked to Janey, and she would love to visit you. Just tell me where and at what time, and she will be there."

George gave her the name of his hotel and his room number. He arranged for Janey to come later in the evening. The woman told him that Janey would go through the services offered when she arrived, and that she would want the payment up front.

On the way back to his room George began to imagine what it was going to be like. Would she do whatever he asked? Would he be able to relax and enjoy it, or would he be too tense? He knew how he wanted it to be.

Back in his room, he had a drink from the mini-bar to help him relax. He took a shower and then lay on the bed, watching some cable TV. He put on his best boxer shorts and a white towelling robe.

It was ten o'clock, and George was starting to wonder if Janey was ever going to arrive. There was a knock on the door. George got up, turned the television off and quickly checked himself in the mirror before opening the door. Standing in the doorway was Janey, the girl on the card. She was even more beautiful in the flesh. She wore a little black dress which was very tight but respectable. On her legs were shear black stockings, well George hoped they were stockings.

"Hi, I'm Janey from the agency, are you George?"

"Yes, please come in, would you like a drink?" George asked, feeling slightly awkward. He wondered what she must think of him. Did she think he was just some pervert who did this kind of thing regularly for kicks, or maybe a sad git who'd never had a girlfriend and was sexually inadequate. Or just maybe she actually fancied him, and would have had sex for free if he'd chatted her up in a bar.

"Yes I will thank you, I'll have what ever you're having," she replied. George poured her a drink. He was beginning to relax; she seemed friendly enough.

Janey sipped from the glass, "Mmm this is lovely, it's making me feel all warm inside. I've got a list of the services I provide. Would you like to have a look and choose which ones you would like?" Janey handed George a small folder that looked like a menu. George opened it and read through the list carefully.

"See anything you'd like?" she prompted.

"Yes . . . but it's all quite a bit more expensive than I had expected . . "

"I know it's expensive, but from our agency clients expect the best and they get the best. I'm sure you will find that it is worth every penny." Janey looked into George's eyes and smiled at him provocatively. He knew she wasn't going to drop the price or even enter into negotiations. If anything this made him desire her more. He certainly didn't want her to leave. He wanted her at any price. He wasn't going to let this stunning woman slip through his fingers for the sake of a few pounds.

"Oh, I wasn't suggesting you weren't worth paying this money for, don't get me wrong, I think you're absolutely gorgeous. It's just that I've never done this sort of

Menu

Straight Massage	£30
Hand Relief	£45
Breast Relief	£80
French	£120
Full Sex	£200
French & Full Sex	£250
Breast Relief & Full Sex	£250

Deluxe Service.
Anything & Everything
you Desire all night
£500

thing before and I really had no idea what the prices would be."

"Oh it's your first time is it darling? Don't worry, we will have a wonderful time. Can I ask if you are a virgin George?"

"Oh no! Nothing like that. It's just that I've been married for a long while. Now I'm separated I want to experience different things, you know."

"Yes, I know exactly what you mean. That's why I love this job. I love experimenting. And I love to devote myself to pleasuring someone and giving them what they want the most. I love pleasing people." Janey smiled again. "Take another look at the menu, I'm sure you'll find something you really want. What would you most like to do tonight?"

George took another look at the list. He didn't want to ask for something that would only last twenty minutes. He wanted to savour the moment. He wanted to feel intimacy with a women again.

"I'm finding it really hard to choose. I'd like to have everything."

Janey pointed to the bottom of the page. "Here is the one for you then. It's our Deluxe Service. Anything and everything you desire, and I'll stay all night. It's by far the best value and because there's so much time, there's no rush. It's the one I like the most. I love it when I have plenty of time to please."

George thought about the prospect of spending so much money on one night. Then he thought of his wife and her lover, and wondered why he was even hesitating. It was his money after all, and he worked damn hard for it. Sometimes sixteen hours and day, seven days a week. She didn't even have a job, the little slut.

"Okay then, let's go for that one. Do you take credit cards?" asked George.

"Oh yes darling that's no problem. We don't expect our customers to have that amount of cash with them." George handed her the folder and she put it in her bag. He found his wallet and gave her his credit card.

"Thank you," she said as she swiped his card through a small hand held machine. George signed. "That's the business over and done with," she said. "I'll have a shower. You can scrub my back if you want George."

Janey got up and walked towards the shower. She unzipped the back of her dress and it slipped off her shoulders and on to the floor. She turned towards George. Her breasts were naked. "What do you think my best feature is George? I've got lovely tits haven't I? All my girlfriends are really jealous of them."

"Yeah, they're gorgeous. I bet they attract attention wherever you go."

"Come over here and help me off with my stockings?" said Janey.

George went to her side and knelt down. He unclipped each suspender and rolled down the stockings. Janey undid the suspender belt and threw it on to the bed. She walked to the shower door, then bent over, slowly slipping her panties over her arse and down her long legs.

Now, completely naked, she stepped into the shower and turned on the faucet. She stood under the spray and the warm water flowed over her body. She threw her hair back and opened her mouth. The water ran in rivulets down between her breasts and over her belly, cascading from her pubic hair on to the shower floor. "This is lovely George, why don't you join me?"

George took off his robe and boxers and stood beside Janey in the shower. She began to lather some soap on George's chest. He stroked her shoulders and ran his hands lightly over her breasts as the water fell over them.

"That feels nice George. Lick them for me."

George leaned forward and began to lick gently around Janey's nipple.

"Ooh, yes George. I love that. My nipples are so sensitive. And the water feels so good on my skin."

Janey handed George the soap. "Will you wash me George? All over." Janey leaned back against the tiles. George lathered his hands and then rubbed them all over Janey's breasts, then over her stomach and down between her legs. Janey turned around. George washed her back and bottom letting his fingers slide the lather over her smooth skin and in between her buttocks. He felt the soft mound between her legs with his soapy fingers.

"Mmmm," moaned Janey, "that hit the spot."

George's penis was fully erect. Janey felt it brush against her bottom.

"Ooh, what's that you've got, you naughty boy! Let me see . . ."

Janey turned round and looked down. "Your wife doesn't know what she's missing."

She took the soap from George and with her soapy hand she clasped his erection and began to massage gently back and forth. "Do you like that George?"

"Yes it's lovely." George opened his legs a bit more. Janey cupped his balls with her other hand while she still massaged his penis.

"It's so hard. I can't wait to get it tight inside me."

She took the spray head and rinsed the soap from George's body, lingering over his erection. Washing away the last of the soap from her own skin she turned the faucet off and reached for the towels. Wrapping one around herself and one around George, she led him to the bed.

Janey lay on the bed. Letting the towel slip down to reveal her breasts. "You love my tits don't you George?" she said. "You haven't taken your eyes off them from the moment I arrived. Do you want to fuck them? I'd love to have your stiff cock between them, with you thrusting into them till your cum spurts."

George undid the towel and it dropped to the floor. His erection pointing upwards.

"Come here George. Straddle me and put that lovely cock between my tits."

George was lost for words, she was everything he had ever dreamed of. He climbed on top of her and she took his hard cock and nestled it in her cleavage. With her hands she pushed her tits together, enveloping his cock between them. George began to push his penis into them, the feeling was wonderful, moist and warm.

" I could never do this with my ex, Kim, she had small tits and she wasn't very adventurous sexually anyway."

"That's a shame George. Now you know what you've been missing."

George's thrusts became more urgent. "Yeah, that's good, fuck my tits. I want your cum all over them George." She held her breasts tightly together as he rode her faster and faster, panting her name with every thrust, "Janey . . . . Janey . . ."

"You're ready aren't you darling. Let it all go, all over me." He started to come. First just a few droplets, then with each spasm his hot cum spurted on to her tits then on to her face as his ejaculation gathered momentum. Janey licked her lips tasting his spunk. "Oooh, that was so good George. When did you last have sex, it must have been a while ago to have so much spunk saved up. You must have been aching for it."

George collapsed onto the bed beside her watching her as she massaged his cum into her breasts. She wiped it from her face and leaned over to kiss his lips. Then she moved down to his chest, caressing and kissing his pink nipples. She slid down further and found his penis still wet with cum and began to lick it. Running her tongue over it, trying to make it hard again. Soon it began to stir back to life, and it wasn't long before she had it's stiff full length in her mouth. Janey sucked it, teasing it with her tongue. George became more and more aroused by her expert technique. Her mouth felt luxurious, warm and tight around his cock.

"I'm going to fuck you now. Lay on your back and open you legs . . . yeah that's right pull your pussy lips apart so I can see. . ." George was getting more confident. He was beginning to think that she really did like him. He was on top of her now, he took hold of his cock and guided it into her pussy, pushing it's full length into Janey's cunt.

"Ooh, your prick is so big I can hardly take all of it," Janey gasped, "Be gentle with me."

George thrust deep into her pussy holding her thighs with his hands.

"Mmm George, that feels so good. Your cock is so hard . . and so big . . . oh!"

George's arousal heightened at her words and his cock began to fill with semen. He powered into her, watching her breasts bounce up and down with every thrust.

"Oh George . . George . . "

His cum fired deep inside her.

They both relaxed on the bed and it wasn't long before they fell asleep.

George dreamed he was sitting in a chair watching Kim and Janey fight over him. They shouted at each other, and then Kim grabbed Janey's hair. They fell to the floor struggling, wrestling each other. Janey pinned Kim to the floor and sat astride her holding down her wrists. Then she kissed Kim passionately, pushing her tongue deep inside her mouth. Kim responded and they began to tear off their clothes in a heated sexual frenzy. George joined them. They took off his trousers and ran their hands all over his body. Janey took his erection in her hand and gently stroked it whispering to him about how beautiful it was and how much she wanted it in her mouth . . how much she wanted him to come in her mouth. She squeezed his cock in her hand and put her lips to it's very tip. She let her tongue touch it gently, but teased and wouldn't take it inside. He wanted it to slide into her mouth. He wanted to feel her sucking hard on it like she had before. She stroked his length again with her fingertips and he felt her sensual soft tongue lightly licking at it's tip. He ached for it to slip inside . .

George woke up. Janey was caressing his erect cock in her hands and running her tongue up and down it's length.

"Good morning George. I just woke up and saw that you had such a lovely erection. I couldn't let it go to waste. I'd love to suck it if I could. Could I suck it George . . . please say I can."

"Yes you can Janey!" George replied, not believing there could be any other answer to such a request!

He watched his cock disappear in between her lips and she looked up at him as she sucked on it. She held it tightly in her mouth with her fingers at it's base, and he watched it sliding in and out as she sucked harder and harder.

"Oh George. I love your cock so much. Please could you come in my mouth?" she purred. "I'd love to taste your creamy spunk. I'd love to swallow it all up. Please say I can . . ."

"Yes Janey," George replied, his cock pulsating at her words. "I'm going to come in your mouth, get ready." Janey grabbed hold of his buttocks as if to brace herself.

"I can't hold back any longer . . . I'm coming . . . Arrrgh . . . Mmmm." George's cum hit the back of Janey's throat. She tried desperately to swallow it all. Her mouth was full as his cock kept pumping into her. He clenched his buttocks, and shuddered as the last drops splattered into her mouth. George looked down to see Janey licking her lips.

"Ooh that was lovely. I'll be able to skip breakfast now," said Janey, still running her tongue over her lips. Janey got up. "I'm just going to take a shower George. Then I had better be going."

George watched her disappear into the shower and thought what a stallion he was; three times in one night. He could see her shape through the shower curtain as she washed her body under the falling water. She ran her fingers over her breasts as she rinsed off the soap. He wondered why he'd never done this before.

Janey pulled the shower curtain back and stepped out drying herself with a big white hotel towel.

"Can I have a private number for you Janey, so I don't have to do it through the agency next time?"

"I'm sorry George, I just can't let you have that. It's totally against the agency's rules and I'd be risking my job. But, I can give you a small catalogue. It lists girls all over the country so wherever you are you'll be able to find someone to please you."

George was disappointed. He'd hoped that Janey would want to see him again. Maybe even as a date. He really liked her, and she'd paid him so much special attention - more than she normally would show a client, surely?

Janey went to her bag and took out a little booklet. She handed it to George. "It's got photos of the girls and they are all really beautiful. They're all clean. Our agency only has the best."

George tossed the book on to the bedside table. Janey took a clean pair of knickers from her bag and slipped them on.

"Do you want the pair I was wearing last night, George, to remember me by." She handed him the panties. "Ooh, they're still warm," she teased.

Janey put on the rest of her clothes. She picked up her bag and went towards the door. "Well George, I must go. It's been great. She leaned forward and kissed his lips.

"I'm sure I'll see you again," said George. "I'm always in this neck of the woods."

"Take care now," she called as she walked down the hallway to the elevator.

George shut the door. He sat on the edge of the bed. All his troubles came back to him and he put his head in his hands. He got up to pack his bags. He had to be out by ten.

As he pushed the last of his clothes into the top of his case and fastened it down, he glanced around to see if he had forgotten anything. He noticed the catalogue that Janey had left him. He picked it up and stuffed it into his pocket; it would be something to read on the journey home.

George left the hotel and headed down to catch the train. There were lots of women hanging around the station entrance, touting for business. None of them could compare to Janey. But deep down he knew that she was just the same as them.

"Want a good time luv?" said a tarty blonde. "It's only twenty."

George hurried on.

He got on his train and found a seat. He stared out of the window. He looked at the business women on the platform, with their smart tight suits and their mobile phones. He wondered how many of them were cheating on their husbands. He wondered how many of them had stepped on men to get where they were. Or maybe they'd just slept their way to promotion.

George remembered the catalogue and took it out of his pocket. He flicked through the pages which were filled with phone numbers and photographs. He looked up his own town in the index and turned to page eighteen. The name at the top of the page was 'Angel'. Underneath was a photograph of his wife, Kim.

"Fucking hell!"

All women are bad.

Bettina writes,

I love this story because I love young men. They can keep going all night! Sometimes it's refreshing to be with someone who hasn't yet experienced everything sexually. Their naivity can be exciting, and it's always a turn on to me to show them things they've never done before.

The Boyfriend

THE BOYFRIEND

As she shut the front door Valerie caught a glimpse of herself in the hall mirror. Idly she brushed a stray wisp of hair away from her face, and straightened her jumper. "You're not bad looking for your age," she said out loud. Somehow the last few hours seemed like a dream. Now would come the nightmare: what on earth was she going to say to Cassie when she got home? She had thought about not saying a thing, but what would she do if Jed decided to come clean? What would Cassie feel then? "Betrayed!" she said loudly frowning into the mirror. It had come from her own lips. Cassie was going to feel so betrayed, and who could blame her. Valerie turned and walked into the kitchen to give the situation more thought as she prepared the evening meal. "Shit," she said, as the vegetable knife sliced her finger and the blood dyed the onion she was cutting a brilliant red. As she rinsed her finger under the cold tap, her mind wandered back to that knock at the door earlier in the afternoon . . .

She had been reading a magazine when she heard the knock and she opened the door to find Jed standing there, clutching a bunch of flowers tightly in his grasp.

"Mrs. Granger . . Valerie, I need to talk to you," he

stammered awkwardly.

She smiled and showed him into the lounge. "Would you like a cup of tea Jed?" she asked, taking the flowers from his clenched hand. "You know that Cassie won't be home for a while, don't you?"

He seemed restless and fidgety. She tried to ignore his hands as he rubbed them up and down his jeans, but she couldn't help noticing the flush of embarrassment creeping up his neck, and his jaw tensing as he tried to pluck up the courage to speak. "Valerie," he said, hesitantly, "I chose this time of day quite deliberately because I knew you would be alone and there's something I just have to tell you!"

He got up from the chair he was sitting in and came over to the sofa to sit beside her. "Valerie, I need you! I've fancied you for ages and I want to make love to you." Suddenly she found herself wrapped in his big strong arms and he was kissing her passionately. She pulled away from his grasp, shocked, and brushed herself down.

"Please Jed, don't. I'm too old for you, and anyway how can I? Cassie loves you. She's my daughter. I can't do that to her. How would she feel if she found out?" She took hold of his hands gently and said softly, "It isn't right love."

She looked into his beautiful eyes. They told her how much he wanted her. It had been such a very long time since anyone had. Something in the back of her mind made her weaken and before long she found herself back in his arms responding to his kisses. Part of her knew it was wrong but she just couldn't resist him, despite alarm bells ringing in her head. "God Jed, this is so wrong, but I want you too. You are so handsome. I . ."

Jed put his fingers to her lips to silence her and his lips met hers. Now his kisses were more urgent and she felt his hands searching for a way under her jumper. As they found her warm breasts she relaxed, and he began to fondle her erect nipples. She felt like a sixteen year old once more, half expecting to be caught at any minute, and the possible risk of discovery made her excitement even more intense. As he pushed her back into the sofa, she could feel his erection straining against her body, and with deft hands she freed his cock from his trousers and began massaging it with her long fingers. He pulled her jumper off over her head and sighed with delight at the sight of her firm breasts. He sank his head between them. Pulling her skirt up over her hips he tugged at her panties and slipped them down to her ankles.

"Valerie, you're so beautiful. I want to have you. I want to play with your pussy, and I want to fuck you."

She could feel the warmth of his body pressing against her as he pushed a finger into her wet pussy and began to play with her gently. His mouth searched for a nipple and he sucked at it. Feelings of ecstacy surged through her as his fingers lingered over her clitoris. She pushed him back slightly so that she could undo his trousers properly and admire his swollen cock. "Oh my God, you're so big and hard. What an erection!" exclaimed Valerie. She knew that she could take him right inside her mouth as this was one activity she had always delighted in. Her head sank into his lap and she took his entire length into her mouth. The tip of his cock pushed at her throat as she sucked him harder and harder. He moaned out loud with the intense pleasure that her mouth and tongue were giving him. She pulled her mouth away and looked up at him, "Is that good?"

"Yeah, fantastic!" he sighed.

Valerie took his penis again into her mouth. Jed arched his back as she gently bit into his straining shaft.

"I want to do it to you to," he whispered. "Let me go down on you. Let me taste you." Slowly he pulled away from her and opened her legs so that he could sink his tongue into her dripping wet cunt. His tongue extended deep into her aching hole and she reached for his cock to hold it tightly, letting her fingers gingerly cup his swollen distended balls. Her gentle touch made him writhe as his mouth ate her pussy.

"Oh yes . . yeah . . that's brilliant. Go on, eat me, tease me," begged Valerie.

Jed found her clitoris with the tip of his tongue and flicked it back and forth.

"Yeah . . that's wonderful . . I can't take much more," she gasped. "I want you to fuck me Jed, now, go on fuck me."

They both stood and she leaned forward into the soft cushions of the sofa, exposing the firm cheeks of her bottom which she held wide apart for him to view her moist pussy. He immediately responded by thrusting his huge cock deep inside her, holding on to her bottom with one large hand whilst the other cupped her breast and pulled at her nipples. She gasped with delight as their bodies locked in unison, and their passions rose towards the final thrust, which sent them both into spasms of ecstasy. Valerie felt his cock burst with energy as his hot cum shot into the depths of her body. They both shuddered as their orgasms peaked together.

They pulled apart and collapsed into a passion-spent heap on the sofa. Arms and legs entwined as their feelings subsided. Their lips locked, and their mouths and tongues softly and lovingly explored each other. Then they lay back not even talking as they came to realise what they had done. Valerie was quite surprised, she didn't feel as guilty as she thought she should. Taking Jed's hand in hers she led him upstairs, "Come on love, let's go and have a bath. It's great together and there's plenty of room for us both."

Going into the bathroom she ran a deep bath, then silently she climbed into the hot water, and motioned for him to climb in with her. He got in behind her and his large hands massaged her shoulders. Her body offered no protest as he soaped her gently, and she relaxed into his strong arms as his hands relieved all the tensions in her neck. Then his hands pushed beneath the water searching for her pussy. Circling her clit he began to arouse her once more. She felt her body climb towards a second orgasm. He pressed his cock into her back as waves of intense pleasure sucked warm water in and out of her cunt as she came. She relaxed again leaning back against his chest and he put his arms around her.

After a while she climbed from the water and wrapped herself in a warm bath towel. Taking his hand she said, "Come on, sit here on the side of the bath," and she patted it with her hand. "Go on that's right. I want to dry your beautiful body."

With the towel she began to dry him tenderly, and knelt in front of him putting the towel around his shoulders. Watching his expression, she leaned forward and took his clean wet cock into her mouth. Quickly he became aroused as her tongue flicked over his shaft. She sucked at him hungrily. His hands stroked her shoulders and he moaned quietly, writhing under her tender touch, as her tongue began licking him more urgently. "Come inside my mouth . . I want to feel you explode there. I want to drink it all. Go on, let it happen. Just let it happen." She sucked harder at his cock letting her mouth tighten around him in a gentle rhythm. She could taste a small drop of salty flavour on her tongue which made her lick him more, cupping his heavy balls in her hands and pulling him even further into her mouth. His cock was throbbing with pleasure as she opened her mouth wider to accommodate him further inside, her back teeth grazing him as she sucked on him more and more. Finally she felt him ejaculate. His hot cum surged into her throat and she drank it down greedily letting him stay in her mouth whilst his orgasm peaked and dwindled in it's warmth.

"God Valerie, you really know how to make a man

feel good. I'd hoped you wanted me." Jed smiled and ran his fingers in her hair as she wiped her mouth. Then he pulled her to her feet and they kissed. He could taste his salty cum in her mouth and he still had the faintest taste of pussy on his lips.

Silently they dried themselves and went down to the living room. They put on their clothes and sat gazing at each other for a few stunned moments.

Jed got up to leave "I have to go or I'll be late, but what are we going to do about Cassie? I don't want to hurt her, but I knew I had to have you."

Valerie shook her head. She didn't want to hurt Cassie either, and she knew how shocked and upset she would be. "I don't know Jed. I'll have to tell her, but God knows how. Leave it to me, I'll think of something."

Although Valerie knew she had done wrong, there was this spark between her and Jed. Their sex had been so hot, she knew she wouldn't be able to resist him any time he knocked at her door for it again.

Valerie dried her hand. The cut had stopped bleeding now and she went to the first aid cabinet for a plaster. Wrapping it tightly around her finger, she heard a key turn in the lock. Valerie felt sick. Her stomach churned as she thought of what she'd done. Cassie hurried through to the kitchen.

"Cassie, I . ."

Before Valerie could say anymore, Cassie interrupted, "Mum, I've just done something awful. You won't believe what I've done."

"Calm down dear. I'm sure it can't be that dreadful. Sit down and tell me what's wrong."

"Well I called round to Jed's house to get something I needed for college. Jed wasn't in so his Dad let me in and we got talking. One thing led to another and I . . oh this is really bad . . I slept with him. What the hell am I going to tell Jed?"

Bettina writes,

This story came about through an advert I pinned up on the notice board in our local University. In the advert I asked for 'Erotic Experiences'. A girl called Jade wrote to me, telling me of an experience she had when she was a first year student. I met with her a couple of times and we wrote the following account together. Jade isn't her real name, which she asked me not publish, as she wants to keep her identity private for obvious reasons.

Skin Flick

SKIN FLICK

My name is Jade and I'm a first year art student at University. As this is my foundation year, I've done a bit of everything - fine art, illustration, photography and computer graphics. But, my real interest is film making, which we have only touched on briefly.

I've been desperate for money lately. I was hoping to get a job in a bar or as a waitress, but there are so many other students out there, and not enough jobs.

At the moment I'm sharing a room in a house with a girl called Elaine. We've become real close friends, because we're both in the same boat; we're both students, have no boyfriends and we're really short of money. Elaine gets some money from her parents, but it's not much, it just covers the basics. I don't see eye to eye with my parents, they wanted me to be a secretary, or a PA or something crass like that. There's no spirit in that. As my parents aren't helping me, my aunt gave me two hundred pounds when I began Uni. She couldn't really afford it, but she's arty like me, and we've always got on really well. She's been more of a mother to me than my real mum ever has.

Elaine and I don't go out much as we can't afford to. We mainly stay in and read books, listen to tapes or look through the free weeklies.

About a month ago, Elaine and I were giggling over the dirty adverts in the back of the local paper. You know the sort: bored housewife likes doing it over the phone; pussy for sale; French lessons etc. When we finally got to the job section, Elaine noticed an advertisement which read:

FILM EXTRAS WANTED
Earn £££££s
Young and enthusiastic -
Pretty girls and muscular guys required.
Ring now for immediate auditions -
Ask for Nick or Cindy.

Elaine and I looked at each other. Here was something we could do, and as well as earning some money, it would be fun. I couldn't help feeling excited about the prospect of being in a film. Maybe I'd get discovered by some big shot film director. Or, maybe I'd learn something about operating a camera, or directing and producing.

I rang the number and asked for Cindy. She told me auditions were taking place all day on Saturday, and to come along around two o'clock.

The next morning all I could think about was the audition, and whether I should prepare something for it. The lady on the phone hadn't mentioned anything, so I figured that they would probably have something for me to read. Maybe they'd ask me to act out a scene with another actor. There were still two days to go until the audition, so I tried not to worry about it.

At eleven o'clock I had a life-drawing class which I always enjoy. We get all sorts of different people sitting for us, who are all different shapes and sizes. We get housewives relieving their boredom, OAP's earning a bit of extra cash, and occasionally we'll get a young attractive person who wants to show off their body. One week we had a girl of about my age called Cherry. She was absolutely beautiful. Her hair was peroxide blonde in loose curls. It fell just above her shoulders and shone in the sunlight that came through the windows. She lay naked on a green velvet day bed. Her body was stunning, well toned and firm. Her breasts were around 34D. I loved the way she had also dyed her pubic hair peroxide blonde, and shaved it neatly. She seriously made me think about becoming a lesbian! I was hoping it was going to be her again so I sat at the front. I wasn't at all disappointed though when the tutor introduced Ben to the class. I had seen him walking around the campus, and thought to myself what an absolute hunk. And now, here I was, about to see him totally naked. The tutor told Ben to change behind the screen. We all looked at the screen for the time he was behind it; all of us waiting to get that first glimpse of his muscular form. The class was silent as he stepped out from behind the screen. The girls were in awe of him, and I'm sure the boys felt a bit inadequate in his presence. There was none of the usual chit chat amongst the students, they all put pencil to paper straight away. I found it hard to concentrate, as being right at the front he was only about six feet away. His big blue eyes seemed to be staring straight into mine. I could see every inch of him, and I mean every inch! I looked at him carefully so I could start to create him on the page.

Then suddenly, I had a really wicked idea. I knew I shouldn't do it, but I just couldn't stop myself. I knew that as I was at the very front, no one else would be able to see what I was doing. I gazed into his eyes and I licked my lips in a really suggestive manner. I opened my legs just enough so that he could see the crotch of my knickers. Then I let my eyes wander down to his flaccid penis. I stared at it, still licking my lips. It was only a moment or two before it started to respond, and a few seconds later it was fully erect. It was a real thrill to know I could control it, when he obviously couldn't. I expected some kind of reaction from the class, but being British, everyone just ignored it and carried on. He didn't look at me again after that.

Saturday came. All morning Elaine and I helped each other to get ready for the audition. We did each other's make-up and chose some really nice clothes to wear. Elaine looked really good in my best red dress. It looks better on her than on me, as she is more curvy with a bigger bust. The colour goes well with her long blonde hair. I wore my cream cotton skirt and my blue chiffon blouse. As the blouse is see-through, I had a small cropped blue top on underneath. Elaine said it looked like a bra but I didn't think so.

The address we had been given was just outside town. We got off the bus and walked up a long, tree-lined road, till we came to some large iron gates. The iron work on each gate was painted gold and black. Embedded in the pattern were some entwined initials. We figured this must be some big shot's house to have gates like these - maybe the star of the film, or the director. I pushed a button on the intercom by the gate, and spoke our names into it. The gates slowly slid open and we walked inside.

A long path led us to a large country house. Parked outside were some limousines, most of which were black with dark tinted windows. We rang the bell and waited to be let in. A woman opened the door to us. She introduced herself as Cindy. She was businesslike and wore a two piece dark blue suit. Her hair was up on top of her head, and she wore glasses that seemed too big for her face. She led us through a high archway, and down a wide hallway lined with sculptured figures of naked men and women, who were involved in all sorts of diverse sex acts. Elaine and I looked at each other. We both must have thought the same thing - what had we let ourselves in for!

We were then ushered to a red velvet sofa in a small hexagonal room, and told to wait. After a few minutes, a young woman tottered into the room wearing the highest stiletto shoes I'd ever seen. Her ample bosom thrust forward as she balanced precariously, and a skin tight skirt showed every contour of her buttocks and thighs. She pointed to a door with talon like, red painted finger nails, and said, "Mr. Harrington will see you now."

Elaine and I got up, slowly walked over to the door, and cautiously I turned the handle. We peeped round the door to see a large glass desk, behind which sat a middle-aged man on a robust cream leather chair, drink in one hand and cigar in the other. He beckoned to us to sit down. We sat opposite him in upright chrome and leather chairs. I felt uneasy.

"My name is Harrington. You must be Jade and Elaine?"

"Yes, I'm Jade and this is Elaine." I replied, trying to smile.

"So you have come in answer to our advert for actresses. Have you any experience?"

We tried to bluff our way, saying we were art students, and that we'd done some acting in film-making classes. I noticed him looking at Elaine. He was looking at her legs, and then her breasts, while she was talking. I thought to myself what an old letch he seemed to be. His large belly strained the buttons of his shirt. His cufflinks were big and vulgar, and flashy gold rings adorned his podgy fingers. He wore far too much gold jewelry around his neck, and what was left of his hair was in a seventies perm.

He turned to me and said, "If the part requires it, would you take off your clothes?"

We were more than a little surprised at this question,

and really didn't know what to say.

"If you want to be actresses, you have to be prepared to do all sorts of things," he continued. "Some of the most famous actresses in Hollywood started in skin flicks."

I looked at him indignantly. I was lost for words.

"The films I make are art films," he said proudly. "They're about young women and their sexual awakenings. Kind of modern day Emanuelles if you like. It would only take a day to film your scenes, and we'd be filming it right here in this house. I really need fresh, new, young faces, and you two are perfect! All I want you to do is say a few lines, take off your clothes, and pretend to have sex with various partners."

I grabbed Elaine by the shoulder and led the way to the door. She was more than keen to follow me.

Harrington laughed, a deep belly laugh. As we reached the door he said, "Listen girls, don't be hasty. You two are just what I'm looking for. Think about it - everyone has to start somewhere. You never know where it could lead. And you haven't heard what I'm offering you yet. It's an awful lot of money . . ."

Elaine paused and said to me, "Let's hear what he's got to offer, it can't do any harm."

Reluctantly I agreed, and we returned to our seats.

"I'm glad you've seen sense," Harrington continued. "Like the girlie said, it can't do any harm to hear me out. I won't bullshit you. I'm going to make you an offer and all you have to do is say yes or no. No pressure. If the answer is no, I won't say anymore, you can just get up and leave."

Elaine and I looked at each other and waited to hear the 'offer', which I was sure wouldn't change our minds.

Harrington leaned forward across the desk, both palms flat on the glass top. "Two thousand a piece," he said, "for a day's work."

I was stunned. Two thousand pounds. No way could I have imagined he was going to say that much. I started to think what I could do with two thousand pounds.

Harrington got up and said he was going to leave us for a few minutes to talk it over with each other. He said he'd need an answer when he came back. As he disappeared out of the door, Elaine and I began to whisper.

"No one need even know Jade. It's not like it's going to be seen by anyone we know. Two thousand pounds is a lot of money. I'm really tempted. What d'you think?"

I couldn't believe that I was considering it, but I was. I thought for a few moments, and then said, "He did say *pretend* to have sex, didn't he?"

Elaine reassured me, "Yeah, he definitely did. Anyway, it's not like we're virgins is it?" she said.

"What if I get stuck with a really ugly fat git. I couldn't stand someone like that on top of me!"

"Just go through the motions and collect the cash," said Elaine.

With that, the door opened and in walked Harrington. Elaine blurted out, "We'll do it!"

"Great!" he exclaimed. "Let's do your screen test, then we'll be filming tomorrow." Harrington lit a cigar and looked really satisfied that he had been able to persuade us. He pushed a button on his desk and in walked the girl with the fingernails. She wiggled over to the desk. Harrington told her to take us to the green room and get us ready for a screen test. She took us both by the hand and led us back down the hallway past the statues to an elevator. As we went down two floors, she looked at herself in the mirrors that lined all four sides. She adjusted her bosom and examined her make-up, pouting at herself as she checked her lip line.

When the elevator came to a halt, the doors opened and we stepped out. The girl took us into a large dressing room full of rails of clothes, piles of shoes and props. She said that Elliot would help us to get ready, and then she tottered out.

We looked around but we couldn't see anyone. On one side of the dressing room was a huge mirror, which covered the whole wall. I sat on a stool and Elaine began to look through some of the clothes on a rail.

"Look at this Jade," she exclaimed, pulling out a rubber cat suit. "And look, it's got a split crotch!"

I got up and went to see. There were four of the same outfit in different sizes. Under the rail were boxes full of various sex toys. There were whips, vibrators, strap on dildos, and many other things that were totally new to me.

"Are you sure we're doing the right thing Lainey?" I asked, holding up a big black dildo.

"Just think of the money Jade. When tomorrow's over

we can pretend it never happened. It's only one day after all."

The door opened and in came a man; I use the term very loosely. His shirt was almost identical to my blouse, and when he saw me he said, "Snap, we have such good taste! We'll have to share our shopping secrets." He introduced himself as Elliot. We told him we were here for a screen test. He ran his slender hands along the rails and produced two outfits. Handing one to each of us, he told us to change into them. Mine was a purple basque, which had small metal clips running down the front, and matching knickers. Elaine was given a black lace halterneck bra, also with matching knickers.

We hurriedly changed, and Elliot took us into the next room. It was huge, with lots of filming equipment set up, and a bedroom scene at one end. A woman was busy unraveling some cables. When she saw us she looked up.

"Hi, I'm Linda. I'm going to video you to see how you come out on film. Don't be nervous, it's going to be fun. You both look really hot in that lingerie, don't they Elliot? Oh there's no point asking him, he bats for the other side!" With that Elliot smiled, made a rude gesture and walked out of the room.

"I'll go through the scene that I want you to do, and then I just want you to do the best you can," said Linda. "On these boards are some lines I want you to say, just so we can hear how your voices come out. So, it will go like this: one of you should be on the bed, Jade, that can be you. Elaine, you'll come in and read what's on the board.

When she's finished speaking Jade, then you read your lines. Then, Elaine I want you to join Jade on the bed and gradually I want you to undress each other. Finally I want you to kiss and caress. When you hear me say 'Cut' you can stop."

Elaine and I looked at each other. Linda sensed that we were apprehensive. "Don't worry girls," she said, "just pretend you're kissing your boyfriends."

We smiled and I said, "Okay Lainey, we can do this." I climbed on to the bed and Linda told us to start when we were ready. Elaine walked across the pretend bedroom towards me. As she reached the bed she read her lines:

"I've wanted to fuck you since I first saw you. I've longed to feel that dampness between your legs, and lick the sweet juices from your cunt."

I looked up at the board and started to read out my response:

"I've been waiting for you. Come over here. I want to know what it's like to be fucked by another woman. I can't believe we're going to do it right now. It's not just a fantasy. Let's undress each other."

Elaine climbed on to the bed and began to unclip the fastenings on my basque. I reached round to undo her halter neck and then pulled it down exposing her young breasts. I was a bit surprised when Elaine started to kiss me so soon. I responded to her kiss and gently pulled her towards me. She finished unfastening my basque, slipped it from my shoulders, and let it drop to the bed. Elaine's tongue started to probe inside my mouth, which I found surprisingly erotic. I began to caress her hair, then moved my hands down to cup her beautiful breasts. I rubbed the soft flesh around her nipples, and they became erect at my touch. I felt Elaine's hands on my thighs and she slowly began to pull down my knickers. I wasn't imagining a man doing these things to me, as Linda had suggested, I was thinking only of Elaine. We both wriggled out of our knickers. Then Elaine started to lick and suck my nipples. This felt wonderful. Almost without thinking, I slipped my hand down between Elaine's legs. Her pussy was soaking wet and I pushed my fingers deep inside. Elaine gasped at my touch.

"Cut!" exclaimed Linda.

We suddenly came back to reality.

"That was a great bit of acting, you'll do fine!" she said, taking the video tape out of the camera.

We went back to the changing room and got dressed. Harrington had arranged for us to stay the night, so as to get an early start in the morning. He sent us home in a limousine to collect some overnight things.

On the way back to our flat we hardly spoke. I was trying to absorb the days events. My thoughts kept returning to what had happened between Elaine and I. It was so unexpected to have such feelings for a friend, who I had never before thought of in a sexual way. The limousine stopped and we went indoors to collect our stuff. We grabbed some underwear, a change of clothes and our toothbrushes and were soon back in the limousine.

On the return journey we were a bit more relaxed. I

desperately wanted to talk about the test but couldn't decide what to say. Elaine helped me out by bringing up the subject for me. "We did a good job today didn't we, in the screen test? We're better actresses than we thought, aren't we?" she said, fiddling nervously with her hair.

"Were you acting all the time Lainey, or did you start to get turned on for real?"

"Did you then?" she replied coyly, not answering my question.

"Well I must admit for a moment there I did get a bit excited. C'mon tell me the truth, you did get into it didn't you?" I said.

"You want to know the truth? I was so turned on from the moment I saw you laying on the bed. You looked fantastic, I couldn't wait to kiss you. Did you notice how I kissed you almost immediately?"

"Yeah, I was a bit surprised. But I really enjoyed it. I didn't want it to end, and when she said 'cut' I felt like telling her to butt out."

"That was just when you put your hand between my legs, and I was soaking wet, and I was wondering what you were thinking of me . . ."

Our conversation was cut short as the car pulled up in the driveway and we had to get out. The girl with the fingernails and the ample bosom appeared at the door. We followed her as she led the way up a wide staircase. We watched her bottom wiggle from side to side as she negotiated the stairs in her stilettos and tight skirt. She showed us to our room for the night and as she left she said, "I hope you find the room pleasing. It has an en suite bathroom and there's a box of toys if you feel playful."

Elaine immediately ran over to where the girl had pointed. She looked in the box and giggled. From it she pulled out a shiny gold vibrator, and looked across at me. "This one matches the decor!" she said, laughing. She was right, there was a lot of gold in the room. It was how I imagine the penthouse suite in the Savoy would look, with plush furniture and velvet drapes. Everything seemed to be trimmed with gold. The bed was circular and it was right in the middle of the room. I'd never seen a round bed before and I jumped straight on it. Elaine had found the drinks cabinet and was choosing something for us. She looked so sexy in my red dress, and at that moment I really wanted her. She poured two drinks and came over to me. I didn't know what it was but it was delicious. It made me feel warm inside.

Taking the drink from my hand, Elaine put it on the side table. Then, she leaned forward and kissed me. At last we could finish what we had started earlier. All the tensions of the day evaporated, and we fell back on to the bed exploring each others bodies. Elaine put her hand under my skirt and touched me through my cotton panties. I lifted my bum up and she pulled my panties off. I undid my skirt slipped it off and threw it on the floor. Elaine was on top of me now kissing me deeply and passionately, running both her hands through my hair. I lifted her dress up so that I could grab her arse and massage it with my fingers while she kissed me. I slipped my hands inside her panties and felt the soft smooth skin of her buttocks. Elaine stopped kissing me and started unbuttoning my blouse. Then she lifted up my top revealing my breasts for her eager mouth. She gently licked my already erect nipples sending waves of pleasure through me. She pulled off her dress leaving just her panties on. I slid my hand down the front of her knickers so that as she straddled me she was sitting on my hand. My fingers found her clitoris and she writhed back and forth, as I rubbed harder and harder, making her squeal with delight. I thought she was going to come, when suddenly she got off the bed. I asked her what she was doing, and she said she was just going to get something from the box. I played with my pussy while I watched her walk across the room. She slipped off her panties to let me see her gorgeous swollen pussy as she bent over the box. She searched through the toys, turned to me and said, "Look what I've found."

"Oooh, a double headed dildo, bring it over here Lainey."

We sat opposite each other on the bed, our legs wrapped around each other, our pussies almost touching. I took the dildo from her and gently eased it into my cunt. It felt delicious. I got hold of the other end and probed and pushed it's head between Elaine's pussy lips.

"Oooh yeah. That feels *so* good!" Elaine said gasping breathlessly. She took hold of the dildo with her hand and began to writhe. Gently moving on to the dildo, her arse slid against the fresh cotton sheets. With her other hand she felt her own wetness, then pushed her fingers into my mouth. I'd never tasted another woman before. I sucked and licked as she ran her fingers over my lips. We stared into each others eyes not daring to blink. We were mimicking each others actions. It was as if we were looking into a mirror. Elaine closed her eyes and leaned back on her hands, lifting her arse and pushing herself further on to the dildo. Her movements became faster.

"I'm coming Jade, I'm coming . . . oooh . ."

Seeing Elaine start to orgasm was such a turn on, and my pussy was so hot, I couldn't hold back any longer. My fingers found my clitoris and I began to rub myself faster and faster until I came. I cried out, the feelings of pleasure went on and on, both of us writhing together.

"Wow that was the best!" I said as Elaine looked into my eyes, smiling. She fell into my arms and we giggled.

Boy was I starving. I always get really hungry after a good fuck. I told Elaine I was going to try to find the kitchen. There must be some food in a fridge somewhere. I opened the door as quietly as I could and made my way back to the stairs. I figured the kitchen was most likely to be on the ground floor. I slipped quietly down the stairs hoping not to be heard; I didn't want to be discovered creeping around the house late at night. I knew that there were lots of rooms off the main hallway so I thought I'd look there first.

I walked past the statues in the dimly lit hall and ran my fingers over the smooth surface of some of them. You know what it's like, when you know you shouldn't touch something, you just can't help yourself. The statue I liked the most was of a women being taken from behind by a really muscular guy. She was on all fours and he was really giving it to her.

Suddenly I heard a noise. It was a kind of grunt that occurred every few seconds. It was coming from a room at the very end of the hallway. The door was slightly open and a shaft of light escaped on to the plush hall carpet. I approached with caution, not knowing what I would find. I peered in, and to my horror, only a few feet away was Harrington, his trousers and pants down round his ankles, and a string vest that didn't quite reach his hairy fat arse. Pressed into his backside were the stiletto heels I'd seen climbing the stairs in front of me earlier on. Their owner was perched on the edge of the desk with her legs wrapped around Harrington. Each time he thrust into her he let out a disgusting grunt. I looked up at the girl's face, her chin rested on Harrington's shoulder. She seemed to be getting no pleasure at all. She may as well have been typing a letter. He said, "You want it don't you . . can't get enough of it can you . . you really love it . . ."

"Yes" she panted.

"You really want my love pump up ya, don't ya girl?"

"Yes" she gasped.

I suddenly realised that she was looking straight at me. My heart began to race. I imagined her pointing across and loudly announcing my presence. Instead, I was amazed when she smiled at me over Harrington's shoulder. I smiled back at her, and stepped backwards intending to leave, but I found myself still watching. I couldn't take my eyes off the girl as he pounded into her.

"You're so tight," he said. His grunting becoming more frequent, his thrusting more urgent.

"Are you ready to come?" he asked.

"Yeah, I'm ready whenever you are darling," she replied, still smiling at me.

"Now!" he shouted out. He thrusted faster, slamming into the girl. She faked an orgasm, panting and gasping for breath.

When he'd finished, he pulled up his pants. The girl slipped off the table and straightened her skirt. "Oooh, that was lovely darling," she said, "you certainly know how to please a girl, Mr. Harrington. No one else can fuck like you can." She was obviously well skilled at pleasing Harrington.

"That'll be all, Miss Kiss," he said as he zipped up his fly. I hid in the shadows of the statues and waited for them to leave. Harrington walked by, his face as red as a beetroot. He disappeared up the stairs. A moment later Miss Kiss emerged and stood in the doorway.

"Where are you hiding, you naughty girl, I know you're still there," she said.

I stepped out sheepishly, with my head down, feeling just a little bit ashamed of myself. Miss Kiss told me to come into the room with her. I followed behind.

"Don't you think it's just a bit naughty to spy on people when they're having sex?"

I nodded yes.

"I am going to have to punish you. Then we'll say no more about it. Come here and lean across the desk. I'm going to spank your bottom."

I did as she told me. She lifted up my skirt to reveal my white panties. She pulled them down exposing my bare buttocks. Then I felt the sting of her hand against my cheeks. Again and again she smacked me. The last smack turned into a caress, and she slid her middle finger between my legs and felt the soft mound of my wet pussy.

"There," she said, "I hope that's taught you a lesson. Now go back to your room. I'll come to wake you when it's time to start work in the morning."

I pulled my knickers up and smoothed down my skirt. As I went to walk out of the door Miss Kiss said, "Aren't you forgetting something?"

I couldn't think what she meant so I just looked at her.

"Aren't you going to thank me? I've been very lenient with you."

"Thank you, Miss Kiss."

"That's better, now off you go."

I went back to my room and Elaine was already asleep in bed. I took off my clothes and slipped in beside her. I drifted off to sleep dreaming of Miss Kiss.

We were already awake and chatting when there was a loud knock on our door at six o'clock. Miss Kiss entered and told us to be downstairs for breakfast by seven.

I cuddled up to Elaine, and put my arms around her. I kissed the back of her neck and caressed her breasts running my hands down to her tummy. She turned to face me, and kissed me. She said that we ought to get up now, but it was so warm, I held her close feeling safe and secure in her arms.

We showered and dressed. The clothes we had brought with us were simple, just a short dress and knickers, as we knew we wouldn't be wearing them for long! We were both nervous and apprehensive about what the day would bring. I kept reminding myself of the money and what I was going to do with it.

There were small signs pointing the way to the breakfast room. We walked past the statues then down a flight of stairs through two small rooms, finally seeing a door marked 'Breakfast Room'. Elaine opened the door and as we walked in I was surprised to see someone I knew. Sitting at one of the small round tables with two men was Cherry, the model from my art class. Elaine and I took some breakfast from the long buffet table. I didn't want to sit too close to Cherry as I thought she might recognise me, and if she did, word might get around the university that I was making porno films. Of course, if she was here for the same reason as us, then it wouldn't really matter.

Miss Kiss came in and told Cherry, Elaine and I that after breakfast she would take us to the dressing room where we could get ready for filming. Cherry got up straight away, so we took one last mouthful of food and quickly followed her. Miss Kiss took us to the same dressing room we had been to the previous day. Elliot had laid out three outfits. He said we were to be dressed like American college girls, virginal but naughty. The three outfits were all very similar, with short skirts, white panties, white blouses and white bras. My skirt was very short and plaid, and I wore short socks and pretty sandals. We undressed and put on our new clothes. I couldn't help looking at Cherry as she dressed. Her breasts were pert and firm, and squeezed into a tight uplifting bra. She looked better than ever. I wondered what the script was going to be, and whether I'd get the chance to kiss her, or even to have sex with her.

"I love your hair Cherry," I said, trying to make conversation.

"Oh, thanks," she said, "I like to keep it blonde as it gets me more work."

"Have you done this sort of thing before then?" I asked.

"Yeah, lots of times. I love sex and this pays good money, so I do it as often as I can."

Our conversation was interrupted by Miss Kiss, "Come on girls, I'll take you through to the set."

On the way she told us what was expected from us during the first scenes of the day. "Forget about everything else filling up your minds, this morning you are virginal, innocent college girls, discovering your sexual desires for the first time, with each other. When you look at each other during the filming, it must be with desire and passion. You ache for each other, and you must be totally involved with the fantasy, ignoring all distractions."

We nodded and said we understood. Miss Kiss lead us up to the top of the house and said we'd be filming in the master bedroom. She opened the double doors and we walked into a huge room with an extremely high ceiling. The room was split in two, with equipment at one end and a typical college girl's bedroom scene at the other. Everything in the bedroom looked fresh and clean and new. Covering the bed was a flowery bedspread which matched the curtains.

Miss Kiss introduced us to the director, Gerry Levi. He was a middle aged man, with greying curly hair, and wore brown corduroy trousers and a yellow turtle neck sweater.

He took the three of us to one side, telling us what the scene was and how it was going to develop. We were college girls, all virgins, experimenting with our own and each others sexuality. He told us that one of us had found a vibrator in our mother's bedroom and was showing it to the other two. Then one of us would decide to try it out, and the scene would progress from there. He told us we must improvise at first, and that he'd tell us to stop if he wanted us to change positions or do things differently.

We went over to the bedroom. Cherry had the vibrator and she tucked it into the drawer of the bedside table. Elaine and I must have looked nervous because Cherry whispered some encouragement to us, "Don't worry, you'll do fine," she said, "just get into the roles and let go of any inhibitions. I'll talk about sex first and you two just join in."

Gerry came over and told Cherry what dialogue to start with. He returned to his chair and signalled to Cherry to begin.

"I'm glad you two have come over because I wanted to show you something. I found it in my Mom's room yesterday. I've hidden it in here."

Cherry reached in the drawer and took out the vibrator. She showed it to us. We acted like we'd never seen one before.

"What's that?" I asked.

"It's a vibrator," said Cherry. "Look, here's the box it was in." Cherry reached for the box and read out what was printed on it, "Just for women, the ultimate stimulation. Guaranteed to give you the best orgasm you've ever had. The vibrating head will drive your pussy wild with it's pulsating movement."

"What's an orgasm," I enquired innocently.

"It's when you have sex and you get a lovely feeling," explained Cherry, "you know, between your legs."

"I get a feeling between my legs sometimes," said Elaine. "It's hot and kind of wet. I get it when I think of Brad in bed at night. Do you think that's an orgasm?"

"No, I don't think so," said Cherry, "an orgasm is supposed to be an intense feeling, really strong. I read about it in a dirty magazine. I read about how you can have one too. It said if a man wants to give you an orgasm he can rub your pussy till you have one. Like this . . ."

Cherry lifted her skirt and slid her hand between her legs. She delicately spread her fingers and pressed the middle one against the white panties, rubbing it up and down in an exaggerated manner to show us what she meant. She was so good at this, and I was beginning to get into my role in a big way. I wanted to touch her pussy and I wanted her to touch mine.

Cherry turned to Elaine and said, "You lie down, and I'll pretend to be Brad."

Elaine laid down on the bed. Cherry lifted Elaine's skirt revealing her smooth thighs and panties. She began to touch Elaine's pussy through her knickers, rubbing gently over the soft stretched cotton. It looked so sexy, as they are both so beautiful. Elaine opened her legs a little wider.

"Oooh, Brad that feels nice. I love you Brad!" said Elaine.

When Elaine said that, I felt sure the director would shout 'cut', but he didn't, so I figured we were doing okay. I realised that we really could do whatever we wanted, so I said the first thing that came into my head, "Who can I pretend to be?"

Cherry looked up at me and answered, "You'll be *my* lover! You're a tall, handsome Englishman, and you do whatever I tell you because you're madly in love with me."

"Yes," I replied, "I'll do anything you desire my lady."

Cherry handed me the vibrator and showed me how to turn it on. It immediately began to buzz. Cherry knelt on all fours so that her bottom was facing me. She pulled up her skirt and told me to pull down her knickers. I leaned forward and pulled the knickers down to expose her beautiful round arse. She parted her legs and I slowly pushed the vibrator up between them, rubbing the head gently against her pussy lips. She let out a sigh. Elaine was masturbating herself, both her hands moving quickly backwards and forwards between her legs. Cherry told Elaine to lift up her bottom so that she could pull down her knickers. Elaine did so, and Cherry slipped off the panties and threw them on the floor.

"No boy has ever seen my pussy Brad, you're the first," said Elaine.

"Now I'm going to lick your clitoris, like they do in my brother's dirty magazines," said Cherry.

Cherry pushed Elaine's legs further apart and leaned forward to push her mouth against the hot wet pussy. Seeing what Cherry was doing to Elaine, I just had to taste Cherry's sex. I dropped the vibrator on the bed and parting her buttocks with my fingertips I pushed my tongue into her. I let it dart in and out, licking and tasting all her sweet juices. Cherry lifted her head from Elaine's cunt just long enough to say, "Oooh . . . you Englishmen certainly know how to eat pussy." Then she returned her mouth to Elaine's clit. As the tongue touched her waiting pussy again, Elaine began to come, her body writhing under Cherry's sensuous attentions. Shuddering with an almighty orgasm she cried out and gripped the bedsheets. Then, as Elaine's orgasm subsided, Cherry began to come, pushing her cunt further into my mouth in little thrusts as I pushed my tongue deep inside her. She was so wet and so hot in my mouth, and my own pussy ached for her touch. She threw back her head as her orgasm reached it's peak. I wanted Cherry to give me the orgasm I longed for. Cherry looked up at me and said, "Lie down." As I did so she picked up the vibrator. She licked the tip of it and then pressed it against my panties, pushing it into my pussy, the cotton straining taut against it. Pulling the panties aside she teased my clitoris till I panted for her to fuck me with it. I grabbed the vibrator and tried to guide it further into my cunt but Cherry held it back, still teasing me. Elaine undid my blouse and opened the clip on my bra. Exposing my breasts she began to bite and lick my nipples and then she kissed my lips, pushing her tongue deep inside my mouth. Suddenly I felt Cherry push the vibrator inside me. Immediately I started to come, my body flushed with erotic pleasure that I had never known before; these two gorgeous girls giving me all their sexual attentions and bringing me to a explosive climax.

The director said, "Cut! That's a wrap girls. And in one take as well - fantastic! Go get some lunch, you deserve it. Be back at two."

Cherry said she'd join us in the cafe a bit later, so we went on ahead. Over lunch, Elaine and I chatted excitedly. We were on a high and just couldn't stop talking about the events of the morning.

I teased Elaine about her improvisation. "I couldn't believe it when you said: 'Oooh Brad . . . I love you Brad!' Where did *that* come from? I nearly cracked up and ruined everything!"

"I don't know," she said giggling, "I just got into the role! What about you then - 'Who can *I* pretend to be?' You just wanted to get your tongue into Cherry's pussy, you *naughty* girl!"

I had to admit I had a huge crush on Cherry. As she came over to us in the cafe, I started to think about her beautiful, neatly shaved, peroxide blonde pussy. I felt myself blush as she came towards me.

"Do you want some coffee girls?" she asked.

We said we did, and Cherry got a jug of coffee from the counter. She sat with us, and poured coffee into big, deep white cups.

"You two did so well today, I'm so proud of you!" she said as if she was our college tutor. I liked the idea of her as my mentor.

A man came over to our table. He was good looking and tall. Cherry knew him and so she introduced us, "This is Jade and Elaine," she told him, "they did such a good job with me this morning. We've never eaten so well have we girls!" We giggled.

The guy's name was Andy, and he was going to be filming with us in the afternoon. Cherry said she was going to be out in the stables shooting a scene with two guys playing stable hands.

Miss Kiss came in and told us all to be on set in ten minutes. Elaine and I went back to the set and to our surprise it was totally different. It looked like a cheap, New York hotel room, the sort that you wouldn't want to stay in. They'd even hung a neon light outside one of the fake windows. It read 'Minx Motel'. Elliot walked in with two new outfits. We were both going to be saucy chambermaids wearing short, black, shiny viscose dresses, with little white aprons. We also wore frilly white knickers, the kind that lady tennis players used to wear, and black stockings and suspenders. Our shoes were black patent stilettos.

We got changed on the set, and as we finished dressing, Andy walked in and went to speak to Gerry. They seemed to know each other already. Elliot gave Andy a small towel, as that was his outfit!

Gerry called us all over, "Andy knows already what he's got to do", he said. "You two girls just respond to him and follow his lead. You are maids who have come to clean the room in the morning. I want you to come in and start to make the bed. Try to do everything in a sexy manner. As you pull the sheets back you'll find a dirty magazine. I want you to both lay on the bed and start to look through it, giggling and pointing out the pictures in it that you like. Then one of you, Jade you can do it, read a section of the text out loud to Elaine. It's the centre pages and we've marked it for you. While Jade reads, I want you both to begin to masturbate. As you do this, I'll cue Andy and he'll appear out of the shower room and join you. When he comes out, you've got to look surprised as you didn't know he was in there. Seeing you two on the bed, he'll have an erection - he hasn't let us down yet! Andy knows what to do from there, but I want you two to be responsive to him, and willing to do anything he wants."

Andy went into the shower room, and Elaine and I went outside the door to make our entrance.

"This is only going to be *pretend* sex isn't it Lainey?" I whispered, still a little dubious.

"Of course Jade," she replied, "although he is rather sexy isn't he?"

Gerry said it was okay to begin, so we opened the door and entered the room. We tidied a few things up, and flicked a duster around. We went to the bed and plumped up the pillows, then we peeled back the sheet. We faked surprise and excitement at finding the dirty magazine, and then we lay on the bed and began to thumb through it. Giggling, we pawed through the pages, making comments and talking dirty about the pictures. At the centre pages I sat up so that I could read the passage that was marked for me.

"Hey, listen to this," I said. "This sounds just like us." I started to read from the magazine, "The two maids knelt in front of him. They took it in turns to suck on his erect penis as he pushed it into one mouth, then the other. They both wondered which one would be lucky enough to have his cum shoot inside their mouth."

As I had been reading, Elaine had begun to masturbate, lifting her short dress and slipping her hand down the front of her panties. I did the same as I continued to read on, "Thrusting into the blonde girl's mouth, he started to come. His hot spunk shot into her throat as she sucked and swallowed. It dribbled out of her mouth and the other girl kissed her so she could taste it too."

Andy stepped from the shower room and we faked shocked expressions. He said, "Like the taste of hot spunk then do you girls?" His erection already bulging under the small towel that was loosely wrapped around him. His hair and body were wet, and water dripped from him on to the floor. He came over and thrust his erect penis towards me. I gripped it with both hands and covered the length of it so it couldn't be seen, and then I pretended to suck on it, my hands disguising the fact that I wasn't really doing it.

Gerry called, "Cut," and we all looked across at him. "Come on girls, that's not really good enough is it? This morning was great, you really got into it. This scene is fine up to this point but I really need to see that cock going in your mouth."

I looked at him not knowing what to say, but before I could think, Elaine chimed in, "I'll do it."

"Great," said Gerry, "let's go from 'Like the taste of hot spunk then do you girls?' okay."

Andy repeated his line and approached Elaine, pushing his erection towards her. She took it in one hand and stroked it looking up into Andy's face. Then she gently pulled it to her lips and licked the tip, running her tongue the length of it's shaft. Andy began to groan and she started to suck his cock, taking the whole length inside her mouth. I moved behind Elaine and slipped her dress down over her shoulders revealing her young breasts. I reached round and played with her nipples while she sucked on his cock. Watching Elaine with his cock in her mouth, sucking on it so sensuously really began to turn me on. I started to wish I had done it for real myself. I knelt next to her, and pulled my dress down in the same way as I had done Elaine's. My nipples were so sensitive they were almost painful. I looked longingly at his cock as it disappeared between her lips. I looked up at Andy and he looked down at me. He took it from her mouth and brought it to mine, pushing it in gently for me to suck on. I circled my tongue around it's tip and then licked it erotically, before taking it in and sucking hard. He thrust backwards and forwards groaning again and breathing fast. Then he switched to Elaine again, then back to me, just like the story I had read out. Then just before he came he withdrew so the camera could see his spunk shoot out all over our bare breasts.

Gerry called, "Cut! That was fantastic. Brilliant, people, brilliant. Well done!"

We cleaned ourselves up with tissues and the 'fluff girl' came across to help Andy get another erection. It wasn't long before he was ready to carry on.

Gerry told Elaine and I to begin to make love to each other with our outfits on, gradually stripping off until we were totally naked, when Andy would join in. We didn't need any encouragement and we began to kiss and touch each other right away. Slowly I unfastened Elaine's suspenders and peeled her stockings down her long legs and slipped them from her feet. I pulled down her panties and removed them. I fondled Elaine's breasts and as we kissed deeply she slid her fingers down between my legs to find my pussy soaking wet. She pulled up my dress and lifted it over my head, then she licked my nipples as she slid my panties off. When we were totally naked and kneeling on the bed kissing, our breasts pressing together, Andy came over to us. He kissed me and then pushed me down onto the bed, parting my legs with his strong hands. He slid his huge hard cock into my cunt and I received it willingly. Elaine played with herself as she watched us. Andy thrust into me and it felt so good. I was totally in his control, at that moment he could have done anything he wanted. I thought about the statue of the woman being taken from behind. And, as if he had read my mind, Andy withdrew and turned me over roughly so I was kneeling on all fours. I eagerly anticipated his touch, and as his muscled legs pressed against my thighs, he pushed his erection back into me. It felt so good. My pussy tightened around his cock and he pressed down on my arse with his strong fingers. As he thrust into me, Elaine moved to lie in front of me with her legs open. I leaned forward to press my tongue into her wanton cunt. It was so wet and I sucked on her clit, making her squirm with delight. She let out little gasps as I teased and sucked her, and she moved backwards and forwards, pushing her pussy harder against my mouth. As I brought her to orgasm I flicked my tongue in and out of her hole and she screamed with pleasure. Andy thrusted into me faster and faster, and just before he came he withdrew, gripping his cock tightly in his hand to shoot his cum which spurted across my arse and back.

"Cut!" yelled Gerry for the final time. "Brilliant, superb, fantastic!"

The crew gave us a round of applause. Even Miss Kiss was smiling at us. We got dressed and prepared to leave and Miss Kiss gave us our cheques.

As I waited for Elaine to finish gathering her things, Miss Kiss slipped a card into my hand, "If you have a free evening give me a call," she whispered. I smiled and said I would.

Bettina writes,

I've left these pages free in case you want to write your own special fantasy. Perhaps if your partner reads it they will make your wish come true . . .

My Fantasy

MY FANTASY

Dear Reader,

Thank you for reading my collection of erotic stories. I hope you have enjoyed them.

If you would like to write to me, send your letters to the publisher's address below, and the kind people at The Collective will forward my mail to me, wherever I am in the world.

I am currently working on my next book of erotica. If you would like to order it in advance of publication, at a discount on the retail price, it is possible to do so from the address below.

Till next time . . .
Lots of love,

Bettina Varese
c/o THE COLLECTIVE
P. O. BOX 10, SUNBURY ON THAMES, TW16 7YG
UNITED KINGDOM

THE
COLLECTIVE

**sugar-coated babies
on a trashed-out trip to nowhere**

**destination
pulp**